CAUGHT BETWEEN A BEAST AND A HITTA

MYSTIQUE

TEXT UCP TO 22828 TO SUBSCRIBE TO OUR MAILING LIST
If you would like to join our team, submit the first 3-4 chapters of
your completed manuscript to
Submissions@UrbanChaptersPublications.com

1

SIREN

"*I* really need a fill." I sighed to myself while staring down at my red, three-inch stiletto-point nails.

After being locked in my beautifully decorated apartment in the projects for two nearly two weeks, I finally found the strength to climb out of my soft bed. Shuffling down the hallway, I stopped and glanced at myself in the huge antique mirror with brass trim, which had been in my family for generations. It covered half the wall and was something I loved to stare into. I was naked, with the exception of a pair of black lace panties. My tribal tattoos swarmed my body and resembled the popular Middle Eastern tattoo called henna. My brown skin glistened with every turn I made in the huge mirror on the wall. Noticing I had lost a few pounds on my self-appointed imprisonment, I sighed.

"Thank God I didn't lose my ass," I mumbled to myself and continued to examine the rest of my body.

Since the age of twelve, I'd been called a 'brick house.' Now, that slight pudge that held residence in my stomach was gone, and my hips and ass really stole the show. Pulling my butt- length black dreads with red tips up into a giant bun on my head, I made my way to the kitchen, opened the fridge, and guzzled half a gallon of orange juice. Wiping my mouth with the back of my hand, I hurriedly removed a large bowl that had steaks marinating and bit into one raw. My strong teeth ripped the flesh apart easily.

"This is why I don't need any pets." I chuckled to myself.

Go two weeks without eating and see if you have time to be pulling out forks and napkins, or microwaving shit! After partially satisfying my hunger, I grabbed my laptop, took a seat, and began pouring through news articles until I found what I was looking for.

TWENTY-NINE-YEAR OLD WOMAN FROM BELLMONT PROJECTS FOUND GUTTED AND MUTILATED IN NEARBY WOODS

"Twenty-nine? That bitch been telling people she was twenty-five! I knew her ass was older than me."

I breathed a sigh of relief when I read that the lazy, racist ass Bellmont PD had no leads as to who could have killed her. They never had a lead on shit, but constantly made it their business to harass the black and brown people that populated the area. That was until the Black Boys started to get more clout. The Black Boys were five brothers that not only ran Bellmont Projects, but three of the surrounding areas. They had a lot of cops on the payroll, and the ones who wouldn't cooperate seemed to come up missing. While powering on my phone, I was able to get a piece of raw meat out of my teeth that was irritating me. Listen, I said don't judge me. Impatiently, I waited for the notifications to pop up, knowing there would be a bunch, seeing as how I'd lost touch with civilization for the last couple of weeks.

"I knew it," I blurted as I stared at the numerous voicemails, texts and social media notifications. I scanned through the text messages first, most of them from my best friend, Gianna. She was trying to fill me in on the most recent hood gossip and hot tea. Gianna wasn't worried because this was not my first disappearing act. We'd been friends for ten years now. We'd been down since we were two fast tail teenagers, sneaking out at fifteen just to go to baller parties. Gee's parents were more lenient than my mom. When I turned eighteen, I found out why my mother was so strict. Trust, I'll get into that a little later. Clicking on my voicemail, my mom's worried voice came through my speaker.

"Siren, you have to stop. Do you know what will happen if people find out? I didn't raise you to be an animal. You're gonna give me a heart attack. I'm having chest pains!" The phone beeped and went into the next message quickly.

"Girl, it was just indigestion this time. I swear next time, it will be a heart attack! Call your mother, child!"

Thirteen more messages, mostly from my mom, were on my voicemail. Knowing my mother, I couldn't help but to giggle. She was dramatic, and it showed from the voicemails she left. Yes, maybe I did need to control my shit a little better. It didn't make sense to call her and hear her mouth. I figured it would be better to pay her a visit and let her know that I was fine. The last message made me bite down on the corner of my lip. Fine ass Damian. Damian Black, that is, as in the youngest Black brother. Damian, aka Baby Black, was twenty-three, two years younger than me. He was tall with light brown skin and eyes to match. He would have a baby face, but his beard made him appear rugged. It was true that he was youngest out of the Black boys. Still, he was the most ruthless of the crew. This nigga had a major in murder with a minor in torture. You would think I would stay away from his ass. If I had the sense I was born with, I probably would. Except, I was listening to his low, deep voice while soaking my boy shorts.

"Sexy Siren...where you been at, ma? The crew need to meet with you sometime this week, and then I need a private meeting with you to find out why you keep disappearing on a nigga? Let me find out you dealing with another nigga and I'm gonna turn into his worst nightmare."

See? I shouldn't be dealing with him. I shouldn't be turned on right now. Now, I was rummaging through my nightstand looking for the biggest vibrator I could find. Fuck my life.

2

SIREN

*T*wo nuts and a cold shower later, and I was still worked up over that voicemail from Damien. Torture is having the finest man on the East coast and not being able to fuck him. Not being able to slide down his big, pretty and smooth dick. I was tempted to go for my trusty vibrator again, until the pounding on my door brought me back to reality. I knew it was Gianna. I could smell her Gucci perfume through the door. No, she doesn't drown herself in it like a cheap whore, but let's just say my sense of smell was out of this world. I was already dressed, rocking some tiny denim shorts, tan gladiator sandals, and a tan silky tank top; cute and simple. I threw open the door for my best bitch. Before I could get a word out, she grabbed me into a tight hug.

"Best friend, I missed you!"

"I missed you too, girl!" I said, muffled inside her embrace. Finally, she released me and stepped back to check me out. Squealing, she shrieked.

"Okay, I see you. Stomach on flat flat!" she said, imitating Drake. I laughed hard because this chick was so silly.

"Girl, shut up!" I yelled between laughs. "You look cute too," I complimented her, surveying her navy blue maxi dress and Michael Kors flats.

Gee was 5'6, slim, and still had some curves. She was light skin, but damn near white. Gee always alternated between her short pixie cut, which was my favorite because it showcased her cute baby doll face. Or, she could be seen rocking her long, bone straight bundles. Today, she was rocking the pixie cut. We were complete opposites in the looks department. Still, we were both bad bitches, and no one could tell us different. I was tall, standing at 5'10. I could have been a model, except I wasn't a twig like those runway models. Curves should have been my middle name because I had a bunch of them. A pair of double D breasts, little waist, wide hips, and a fat ass. I looked like I worked out on a regular basis, but I didn't. It was just good genes, I guess. I had big slanted eyes, a button nose, high cheekbones, and full lips.

I always got that "you foreign" bullshit. Fuck boys always acted like a black woman couldn't just be exotically fine without being mixed. Fuck outta here!

"Let's go to Talons, and you can fill me in on what I missed." Grabbing my Louis Vuitton backpack, we headed out of my building.

The smell of urine in the hallway pissed me off. I could hear the neighbors arguing next door as we walked past. Babies cried somewhere not too far off. Stepping out the building for the first time in weeks, I was blinded by the late August sun. Quickly, I grabbed my Prada shades from my backpack and slid them on, just as the local d-boys started their thirsty shit.

"Damn, y'all fine as fuck!" one called out to us.

"Dreads, let me holla at your tall ass. A nigga like to climb trees." That last comment had me and Gee dying with laughter.

We both stopped walking, and I removed my shades so I could look this nigga in his eyes. Seeing us stop, one of the dudes ran over to Gee while the tree climber made his way over to me.

"I see I made you smile. What's your name, sexy?" he asked, slowly looking me up and down while licking his lips.

He was cute and had a little swag, but I wasn't interested. I was sniffing him out and could tell that he wasn't an alpha. I had a thing for alpha men, and he definitely smelled like beta. I'd be too much for him. Poor thing.

"I'm Siren, and you are?" I questioned, uninterested.

"Drew. I never seen you around here before."

Was this nigga new? This was my stomping ground, I grew up here.

"Maybe, I don't wanna be seen, Drew, I stated, fucking with him.

"Yo, Drew! Nahhh! That's Damian chick. Fall back." Drew's eyes got as big as baseballs when his little friend informed him of who I fucked with.

"Oh shit! I didn't mean no disrespect, Siren," he apologized with his head down while backing up.

I swear, if this nigga had a hat on, he would've taken it off and put it over his heart. Shaking my head, I turned and walked toward my Benz truck. See? I knew a beta when I smelled one. I hopped in and inhaled the new car smell while I waited for Gee to finish talking. Now, I know you probably got a few questions by now, so I'll take this opportunity to fill you in on a few things until Gee comes.

My mother is a sorceress and my father, may the gods protect his soul, was a shifter. Which makes your girl half-witch and half-wolf. No one knows about the shifter side of me besides my mother, my brother Mike, and Gee. Reason being, there are pure blood shifters around who despise half-bloods. My father actually died fighting his own pack to protect me, my brother, and my mother, which is why I'm supposed to never show the shifter side of myself. Sometimes, I couldn't help it. When I got upset, it was hard to control. I started cramping, which was period cramps on steroids, which just made me more upset and before I knew it, some random person's liver was in my mouth. Lord, I loved me some liver. Thinking about it had me hungry.

I watched as bestie slid in the passenger's side with a huge smile on her face.

"He was cute. Almost as cute as your brother." I made a gagging noise.

"Eww, girl. Mike seen us when we was ratchet ass kids. I remember you used to come over and follow him around the house. For a minute, I thought you was using me to get to him," I said, pretending to be hurt.

"Shit, bitch I was!" My jaw dropped before Gianna burst out laughing. "Girl, you know I love you!"

Sucking my teeth, I peeled off, blasting Kanye West's hit song "Monster."

"Ok, boo. Let me pour you a cup of tea," Gee said, reaching over to turn the radio down.

"Aww shit." I said, ready for the latest gossip.

"Remember stuck up Simone that had the baby by Ray Ray? Well, come to find out, the baby not his, but his twin brother Day Day's baby. This nigga went crazy and beat the shit outta Simone. Now, he in jail."

"Oh shit!" I yelled.

Gee nodded. "Yup, shit crazy. And James, drunk James, girl this nigga done hit the numbers and left the PJs. You know niggas was planning to rob his ass. I'm glad he left when he did." I nodded in agreement.

"I hope his ass go to rehab too!" I replied, making us both laugh.

"Soooo..." Gee cleared her throat. "Last time I saw Shamira... ALIVE... was at the black party when she decided to tell you that she was fucking Damian...." She allowed her voice to trail off, and I could feel her beady eyes staring a hole in the side of my head. It was obvious she was waiting for an explanation. Sighing heavily, I replied.

"That bitch was disrespectful. She straight up knows me and Damian are together, and she thinks it's conducive to roll up on me at my man's party and tell me. Not only is she fucking him, but she fucking him raw and think she's pregnant. Where they do that at? Bitch, I think not. So yea, I killed her."

Listen, I'm not trying to sound petty. It's not like I go around killing people because they stare at me wrong. I don't fight over men, I only kill when I get upset and can't control my anger. Once I'm at that level, the beast takes over and I lose control. Afterward, I had to lock myself away for a while, until I'm sure the rage has subsided. I would never hurt an innocent person. It was so hard for me to control my urges because I was never trained to control or tame them. No one was supposed to know what I was, so who would train me? My brother was better with controlling his. That's because he had six years with my father before he was killed. He was killed when I was a baby, so the only memories I had of him were what came to me in small pieces of my dreams.

We pulled up in front of *Talons*, a black owned nail salon that we loved. I actually drove forty-five minutes out of the way to get here. It didn't matter to me how far this salon was; this black business was going to get my money.

"Gee, stop judging me." She had been quiet ever since I told her I killed that stank hoe.

"You know I hate when you do that dumb shit. You trying get discovered? Not to mention, that bitch is gross." She spat.

"Gee, it's a lot of shit you do with your mouth that's just gross, but I don't judge you." We both stared angrily at each other, until she broke out in laughter.

"Hoe, I can't with you." She rolled her eyes and hopped out the car.

Heading inside, I noticed that it was a quiet day. There were only four people ahead of us. Looking around I spotted Jamilla, my nail tech.

"Hey, Milla. When you gonna be free?"

The chubby, fiercely dressed nail tech looked up from the gel manicure she was currently doing.

"Hey Si, hey Gee! Y'all just give me ten minutes."

Nodding our heads, Gee and I sat down. Gee flipped through the design booklet while trying to decide on her nail choice, while I sat there trying to get rid of the dried blood that was accumulated under my nails. Anxiously, I started trying to get it out. Would you believe I did this for a whole five minutes before I had the bright idea to just go to the bathroom and squirt some of that dial soap under my nails?

As I stood up to head to the bathroom, I heard someone yell out in the nail shop.

"Ohhhhh, girl look. It's that fine ass Damian!"

"Bitch, where?"

I watched as these two thirsty thots squealed and cheered over my damn man. My eyes followed the bug-eyed bitch's finger as she pointed out the window to Dame's fine ass propped up against my truck. He was rocking some gray joggers, showing off a thick print, and a white fitted Polo tee. White Christian Louboutin sneakers adorned his feet. His neck and wrists were heavy, as usual, with jewelry. The sun flickered off his jewels, creating a halo effect around his upper body. I could tell he was fresh from the barber shop because his lineup was sharp, and his waves were making me dizzy just standing here staring at them. From where I stood, I could smell his *Armani code* cologne from here. I didn't know if it was love or lust, but I was craving to feel this nigga inside of me. I could feel my thong melting off my body from the heat I was producing. Focusing in on his face, I noticed that he was staring right at me. The look in his eyes was neither love nor lust; it was pure fucking rage.

"Um, I'm 'bout to go out there and switch my cute ass all around," the treasure troll-looking one with the red, spiky hair told her friend. Gee shot the girl a nasty look, then glanced at me.

"Ouch, my nail just cracked right down the middle!" Treasure troll screamed out in pain.

So, maybe the witch in me could be a little petty at times. At least I didn't kill her– this time. She would live to fight another day out this bitch. Gee smirked at me while Treasure troll ran past us holding her finger. I gave her a shrug and told her I would be right back. I switched my cute ass out the door. His face softened slightly when he saw me standing there. Pushing himself off the truck, he made his way over to me. The first time I met Damian was two years ago.

We were at one of the summer basketball games around the way. Gee just had to drag me out there, and I'm glad she did. Damien was with a group of fly niggas, and we had walked right into each other. My head was too busy in my phone, so I didn't see him walking my way. Except, his ass was looking straight at me, so I knew he did it on purpose. He bent to pick up my poor cellphone that lay flat on the concrete. A girl was pissed because the screen of my phone shattered.

After inspecting the phone, I finally stared up at him and was prepared to raise hell, even though I was at fault. All my words were caught in my throat as I stared into the deep pools of honey that he was passing off as eyes. He smirked, knowing the effect he had on me, and ran his hand over his beard while eye-fucking my body.

"Damn. My fault, shorty. I'll replace that for you. Put your number in my phone so I can contact you and we can go pick out a new one," he told me while confidently handing me back my phone. I paused for a minute, knowing that as bad as I wanted to have sex with this man, I would never be able to. The minute I had sex with a male, I would lose all my witch abilities. At that moment, I was ready to risk it all. It seemed like everybody was watching and waiting to see what I would do. I softly took the phone from him while trying to ignore the chill that ran through my fingers as they accidentally grazed his.

Quickly, I stored my name and number in his phone. He looked at his screen for a moment before looking at me again.

"Siren?" he asked. I nodded my head. "Sexy Siren. My name is Damian. Make sure you answer when I call," he told me in that deep low voice of his.

I nodded again since apparently, my vocal chords were of no use to me at the moment.

"You smell good as shit too..." He leaned in and whispered in my ear.

"Grapefruit," I managed to get out. You could always find me wearing some type of citrus scent when I went out. I didn't particularly care for the smell, yet the citrus stopped the pure blood shifters from smelling my scent.

We parted ways, and I made sure to slowly shift my hips from side to side. After a few steps, I stared back and this nigga was still in the same spot, hypnotized. Got 'im. When he realized I was looking, a slow smile spread on his face, and I'll be damned if a dimple didn't pop up. We hung out for months after that, doing nothing but deep tongue-kissing and heavy petting. He thought I was a good girl trying to take things slow. Little did he know, I wanted to be his nasty freak, his whore, his dreams and nightmares combined, all in one. One night, he took me to an expensive restaurant and afterward, we went to a secluded spot near the woods to chill. He told me that it was his place to go whenever he wanted to chill and think about life. We sat there quietly, holding hands and staring up at the stars. I fell in love that night and knew that life was officially about to be a pain in the ass. Once we made it back to his three-bedroom home on the outskirts of the hood and I saw that Marsean— the second to youngest out of the Black brothers and the one Dame shared the house with— wasn't home, I knew he had something was planned.

Grabbing my hand, he led me upstairs to the bathroom. I bit my lip as tears escaped my eyes while they darted around the room. There were rose petals all over the floor, sink, and floating on top of the bubble bath that was prepared for me. A bunch of grapes and two full champagne flutes sat on a silver platter. My eyes and pussy were leaking something terrible.

"Get in."

Carefully, I stepped out of my pumps and unzipped my dress, letting it fall open and down, forming a tiny pile at my feet. It left me with nothing but a lavender silk thong. Before I could hook my fingers into the sides, Damian was doing it for me. He kept eye contact the entire time and the minute he peeled those sticky panties off me, I could smell my own arousal.

It was obvious that he could too because his dick kept bumping my stomach through his slacks. He stepped back, admiring my body while I shyly looked down. It was the first time I had been completely naked in front of a man. Instantly, my mind went to the three dimples of cellulite on the back of my left thigh, right underneath my butt cheek, and the chipped polish on my pinky toe that rubbed off from my pumps, and the fact that although I shaved the previous day, due to my hair growing extremely fast, I already had a little stubble on the back on my legs. I wasn't even a full-blood human woman, but I was having human woman problems. He lifted my chin.

"Why you looking down? Don't do that, ma. You perfect."

I think, for the first time since I undressed, I took a deep breath in and gazed into his eyes. He quickly scooped me up like I weighed next to nothing. A girl like me was 5'10 with some meat and curves on her bones. Here I was, naked and being cradled in this nigga's arms, like my big ass was a newborn.

He gently placed me into the tub, and I was surprised that the water was still warm. It also let me know he had his brother help him with this while we were out earlier. I gathered my dreads and started to pull them up onto my head. Damien grabbed my wrist, stopping me from pulling them up upon my head.

"Leave them down." My hands dropped like I was on voice command.

He pulled a stool over to the tub and sat while grabbing a bar of soap. This man began lathering my body up with this soap. Nothing was left untouched, besides my pussy, which he left for last. He slid his hands in the water and softly began rubbing. His fingers dove in and out while his thumb pressed my clit. I threw one leg over the side to give him easier access, which he took full advantage of by digging his fingers deeper, causing me to throw my head back and soak in my impending orgasm. What started off as one of the best nights of my life ended in a massive argument once he found out I wasn't going to let him fuck. I even told him about me being a witch and the rule, which I labeled the cock-blocking rule. I seriously wanted to curse whoever came up with this shit. It was probably some overprotective warlock father or something. Of course, I had to prove I wasn't crazy, so I had him light some candles so I could call up some spirits.

I only called on some petty ancestors, not wanting to bother the stronger ones because my boyfriend thought I wouldn't fuck him because I was secretly married or something. My petty ass cousins, they live— or didn't live, rather— for this shit. Man, they showed out. Opening and closing windows, throwing shit around, playing with the lights, even showing themselves in the mirrors.

"Nigga, you bet not do nothing to hurt my little cuz, and stop trying to fuck her!" my cousin Kevin's voice boomed loudly.

Dame looked like he'd seen a ghost. Technically, he had.

"Kev?" Dame asked and stepped a little closer to the mirror. Kevin was my family on my mother's side who had been gunned down a few years ago.

"Yeah, nigga. What's up? How life been treating you?"

"Aww man, a nigga can't complain, still getting to a dollar. How you been?"

"Man, just chilling. Mostly over my baby mom crib checking on my daughter. You wouldn't believe the fuck niggas this bitch be having in the crib..."

"Umm, excuse me. I hate to break up this reunion, but me and Dame were in the middle of a discussion." I spat, irritated while covering myself with a sheet. The nerve of these niggas.

"Well damn. You called me, and a nigga hungry as shit," Kevin complained. Sucking my teeth, I pulled on one of Damian's tee shirts and headed for his kitchen. "But anyway, my nigga," I heard Kev continue as I walked out.

I banged around the kitchen, looking for something to make Kev and the others something to eat. All I could find were some chicken wing platters. I fixed it real cute on a clean plate, poured a glass of water, and headed back upstairs. Would you believe these dick heads were now discussing some video game? I placed the plate and glass in front of the mirror.

"Thanks, Kevin. Now, make yourself scarce!" I spoke loudly over their conversation. He frowned his face up, looking at the old fries on the plate.

"No ketchup?" he had the nerve to question.

"KEVIN!!" I yelled.

"Fine. Thanks, cuz. Love you!"

"I love you too!" I said, blowing out the candles as he disappeared out the mirror.

3

SIREN

*S*o, here he was, crossing traffic to get to me.

"What the fuck is up with you, Siren? Where the fuck you keep disappearing to, huh?" he yelled in my face once he got to me.

"What you worried about me for? Worry about your bitch, Shamira!" I yelled.

I was hot as the memories of that bitch's smug face replayed in my mind. This was the thing. I knew Dame fucked other bitches since he couldn't fuck me. As long as he always strapped up and I never heard anything about it, I was cool. Well, I wasn't cool. My heart shattered more and more whenever I smelled a bitch's perfume on him, but I tolerated it. Having a bitch throw the shit in my face turned me into a whole different monster. Literally. Damian straightened his back and his face fell a little, a sign that I'd struck a nerve.

"Baby, I was just fucking that bitch. You know I'm only emotionally invested in you. That bitch wasn't shit to me. Besides, she's dead. They found her gutted in the woods." I tried my hardest to fake emotion.

I hoped that shit worked, 'cause in reality, I damn sure gave zero fucks. He pulled me into a tight embrace and whispered in my ear.

"I think it was one of the shifters." Damian and his brothers knew about the *others,* as I called them.

The *others* were the shifters, witches, vamps, aliens, and other races of beings that existed among us disguised as humans. Even pointed out a few of the others who had made it to celebrity status. They just didn't know that I was a shifter as well.

"Since when the shifters start killing humans?" he asked. The shifters had always killed humans, but they left no remains. They ate everything, bones and all. It would just look like a missing person's case. The few times I'd killed, I burned the remains because I wasn't eating the bones. With Shamira, I was definitely sloppy. Not to mention, I was still half drunk when I ripped that bitch apart then hopped from tree to tree until I landed behind my building.

The usual crack heads were out, so I grabbed the biggest one and ripped his shirt over his head. Afterward, they all scattered, screaming about how so and so had sold them some bad shit. I shifted back into my regular form and pulled on the crack head's shirt since I shifted naked. I destroyed my cute little black Gucci dress when I shifted the first time, and I was mad. It had cute little designs on it and everything. I mourned my dress for a few, then quickly dipped into my building. Soon as I got inside, I tossed the crack head's shirt and hopped into the shower.

"They usually don't," I said, not wanting to give away all the secrets from my world.

He shrugged. "Long as those fuck niggas stay away from me and mines, I don't give a fuck, you feel me? Which is why I don't want you walking in them woods by yourself no more."

"Dame, you know that's where I meditate. It's quiet there," I stated.

He sighed. "If you would just let me move your stubborn ass out the projects, you would have plenty of quiet."

I had designer clothes, drove a Benz truck, and still lived in the hood, and was proud of it. I grew up here, so this was home for me. Not to mention, a lot of my family and friends were here. To just keep it real, I loved the hood drama. It was entertaining. Eventually, I planned to move and get one of them big ass cribs up in Bellmont

Hills, close to where Mike moved our mother. Mike, my brother, owned a chain of gyms he planned on expanding called *Beasts train harde*r. He sold these energy elixirs that the witch part of him created that got these humans all pumped up. It was like an undetectable steroid. I'm like an oracle to the Black brothers. I go to their meetings, listen to their next plan of attack, use my limited physic powers, and call on the spirits to see if their moves are wise or if they should take a different route. I hadn't steered them wrong yet, which was why they were able to take over the area so quickly. They paid me very well and because of that, I could afford some luxuries while living in the projects. They paid me so well that I could probably live comfortably for the rest of my dry ass, no dick-getting life.

Not to mention, being the girlfriend of Baby Black, I was spoiled to death. Like the truck he just copped for me not even a month ago. He came out of his pockets without me even having to ask. Let's not forget that he hadn't even had a sample of this pussy, and he was doing all of this. Eventually, I'd like to start a business. I didn't want to be some drug dealer's fortune teller forever. I just needed to figure out what my niche was.

"You know I want to start getting myself established first. Right now, I'm just stacking until I feel comfortable."

Rubbing his hand over his beard in frustration, he spoke. "You can keep stacking. I'll get you a house today."

"Oh, you want to move me out to the boondocks so you can be free to fuck all the hood rats?" Now, I was just being petty because I felt some type of way.

"You know what... I'm not talking to you right now 'cause you gonna make me kill you out here in these streets. You really need some dick 'cause you outta pocket!" I knew I was being petty and all; however, his little comment was a low blow. This nigga knew how bad I wanted to get dicked down. He wasn't shit for that comment he made toward me.

I narrowed my eyes. "You're right. Maybe I'll risk it all and go find some dick. This cute dude did try to holla earlier—"

Before I could finish my sentence, he had me jacked up by my backpack straps and slammed me up against the side of the wall facing away from traffic. The pain from hitting the bricks shot through my shoulders and for the first time, I saw his murderous rage focused in on me.

"Listen to me, and listen good, Siren. I think you must have lost your fuckin' mind talking to me like that," he spoke through gritted teeth while never loosening his grip on me. "I will kill you before I let somebody else have you. Everybody in these streets know you belong to me, so if any nigga is dumb enough to fuck you, he's gone."

Someone with an ounce of sense would be done, right?

"Yes, daddy," my dumb ass replied with juices running down my legs.

I knew he couldn't kill me, even if he really wanted to, so that was my reason for not being scared. My response must have been what he wanted to hear because he smiled. It was something he rarely did. I watched as his dimples exposed themselves and he loosened his grip on me. Damien bit my lip lightly before sticking his peppermint-tasting tongue inside my mouth.

"Go on and get your nails done," he told me and reached into his pocket, handing me a knot of money. "I'll see you tonight. Be ready for your nigga."

4
_____

SIREN

*L*ike requested, here my ass was, ready for my nigga. I cleaned up, showered, cooked— hell, I even had L.L. Cool J's *"hey lover"* playing in the background. My dreads were down and swept away from my face. I had coconut oil rubbed into every inch of my skin. Here I was, sexy, soft, clean and wet, looking like a snack. It was about eight-thirty when he knocked. I opened the door without even looking because that Armani Code was wafting through the door cracks. Standing in the doorway with my purple lace bra and thong set had Damien licking his lips. He stepped in and kicked the door closed. He reached for my bra and immediately ripped it off. I didn't know why I tried to get all sexy; this nigga never let my cute lingerie be great. His juicy lips wrapped around one of my stiff nipples while I ran my hands over his deep waves.

Letting out a soft moan, I whimpered, " I cooked."

"Later," he mumbled, switching to my left nipple and pushing me further into the apartment until my heel got caught on my colorful Persian rug. It caused me to fall back onto the white leather couch. Dame's heavy body on top of mine caused me to sink deeper into the pillows. He lifted his head as he looked me in the eyes, showing the intensity of a man on a mission.

I studied him for a brief second, trying to hear his thoughts. Desire was his first thought, followed by love and then finally, there it was... regret. These were always his thoughts when we were skin to skin. I knew Dame loved me, but I also knew he regretted it. Sometimes, I thought it would be best if we separated to alleviate the torture we caused each other. We were like star-crossed lovers, for real. It made me wonder if we were even supposed to be together. I unintentionally sighed, causing him to look up once more.

"Stop doing that. I don't regret loving you," he lied. We had this conversation numerous times.

Nodding my head, I decided to let him have his lie, not wanting to mess up the mood. My urgent desire for some head was a more pressing matter than my need to argue at the moment. Gently, I pushed his shoulders, signaling him to go down. He chuckled before granting my wish and sliding down my body. Once he removed my panties and spread my legs as far as they could go, he lapped up my stickiness. If I could've unscrewed those bitches and tossed them to the side, I would've.

"Hey, pretty. You missed daddy?" he said, speaking directly into my pussy.

She gave her usual response by drooling. Expertly, he eased a finger in and out while using his thumb to smear my juices over my clit. Whimpering, I tried to grind my body down, searching for more stimulation. Knowing what I needed, he added another finger inside and sped up his pace, hitting buttons inside my body like a pinball machine. Grabbing one of my legs with his free hand, he pushed it up into my chest. I wrapped my hand around my ankle and pulled it back until my heel rested right near my ear. Shit, I didn't want nothing in his way, not even my own leg. This nigga was a pussy monster. When he moved his thumb off my clit and replaced it with his warm mouth and began to suck, I screamed out and tried to sit up a little to ride his face and fingers. I could feel every part of my body clenching up, preparing to ride this wave.

"OH GAWWD! FUCK!" I yelled once he slipped his pinky in my

ass. He was like a fucking tentacle monster down there, and he was sucking my soul out of my little clit.

"Come for daddy," he whispered to my pussy. I let my leg go, flung it over the back of the couch and grabbed the back of his head while I slithered my body over his tongue and fingers like my life was depending on getting this nut. I could hear my bones cracking... wait...

"WHAT THE FUCK!" I screamed. My body was trying to shift.

This had never happened before. I was confused as hell, but still wanted my nut so I struggled to hold back the beast as I released my orgasm.

"Ahhhhhh!" I yelled, jerking and twisting and trying to push this greedy nigga away from my pussy. "Fuck!" I placed my shaky hands on my chest, willing my heart to slow down.

"Damn, that was intense," Damian said lowly while licking his lips. He looked up at me, and I watched his eyes grow wide.

"What?" I yelped, scared to death that I may have partially shifted. I quickly glanced at my hands and looked down my body. Still human.

"Your eyes are bright yellow!" he mentioned while still staring at me.

I jumped up quickly, but my legs felt like Jell-O so just as quick, I fell right back down on the couch. Laughing loudly, he put up a finger, signaling for me to wait. I listened to him rummage around the apartment while my mind went into overdrive, trying to figure out what just happened.

I was drawing blanks all over the place when Damian reappeared back in front of me, holding a hand mirror and a warm rag. I quickly wiped myself with the rag and then glanced in the mirror. Sure enough, my normally brown eyes were glowing bright yellow— the color they changed to when I took wolf form. I blinked hard, trying to change them back. I opened one eye and peeked. Still yellow.

"How did that happen?" He continued with his questions while touching my face.

"I don't know." I whined.

"You think they will change back?"

"Yeah... I'm sure they will. Let's smoke," he said. He was so used to my weirdness that when something ridiculous like this happened, he treated it as if it was the norm.

Picking his jeans up from the floor, he searched his pockets for the blunt. Soon, the whole place smelled like loud as we smoked and geeked while watching *The 40-Year-Old Virgin*. I know... painfully ironic, right?

"Yo, that's gonna be you," he hollered while holding the smoke in his lungs. Sucking my teeth, I smacked him in the face with a pillow, causing him to choke on the smoke.

"That's what you get!" In one quick second, he leapt on me, tickling me until I couldn't breathe.

"You think that shit funny?" he asked as I squirmed to get away.

"No!" I screamed while he continued the torture. When I had enough, I kicked him off me with strength he didn't know I possessed.

"Damn, Siren! What you been drinking, that shit your brother be pushing?" he asked.

"No! You know I hate being tickled! But ummm, I think it's time for me to repay you from earlier," I said, glancing at his dick, trying to keep his mind off the fact that I just kicked a 250lb man across the room with one leg like it was nothing.

I licked my lips and watched his dick come alive before my eyes. He loved my head and would brick up at the mere mention of it. The fact that I was part shifter meant my jaws were strong as fuck! So, I dropped to my knees, pulled my dreads up in a ponytail, and prepared to give him this sloppy top.

I HAD DRAINED DAME, so I fixed our plates and brought them into the living room. While we ate, he told me about the meeting Malachi, the oldest Black brother, was requesting.

"So, we need you to be there Wednesday at ten," Dame said in between bites.

"I'll be there," I responded, wondering what the hell they were trying to do now.

"Your eyes are almost normal again," he told me, glancing at my face. I picked up the hand mirror that was still sitting on the table and examined myself. My eyes had mostly returned to their normal reddish-brown color, except for the little flecks of yellow that dotted the edges. I placed the mirror next to me, deciding not to respond about my eye color.

"Are you staying the night?, I asked, starting to feel tired. He shook his head.

"Nah baby, I got shit to get together before this meeting, but I'll call you tomorrow." He stood, going in his pockets and retrieving another blunt, which he placed on the table— something he always did because he never wanted me going out looking for weed.

Walking him to the door, we tongue-kissed before he dipped out. After locking the door, I headed to my bedroom to grab my kimono robe. The silk feels so good against your skin; trust me, go 'head and get you one. Because I can't stand a dirty house, I hurriedly walked back out to the living room to gather the dirty dishes and clean up for the night. While scrubbing the dirty pans and plates, my mind wandered back to the incident from earlier when I damn near blew my cover by shifting. I still couldn't figure out what that was about. A loud howl caused me to drop the glass I'd been about to wash. It shattered at my feet. The sound had come from the woods behind the building. I listened intently, but it was so quiet now it made me wonder if I had imagined the noise. Glancing at the digital clock over my stainless-steel stove, I saw it was a little after midnight. Grabbing my phone, I called the one person who might be able to shed some light. I waited with baited breath until she answered in a sleepy voice

"Siren, what's wrong?"

"Hey, Mom! Nothing's wrong... I just, umm...I just wanted to ask you some questions..."

"Questions about what? Where have you been? You know I read

about that girl they found behind your building," she said, fully awake now.

"Ma! Slow down! I meant to come see you today, but I got distracted. Listen, I almost shifted in front of Dame tonight. I don't know why. I wasn't angry or anything. I managed to control it though, but my eyes. My eyes glowed for hours afterward. Do you know what's going on?"

She was silent for a minute. "Um hmmm... and what were you and Dame doing when you felt the shift?" My face heated. No way in hell I was going to tell my mom that I was on the verge of busting a toe curling nut when I felt the shift.

"Talking," I lied.

"Yea, right. Siren, I'm not stupid, although I was a stupid ass twenty-five-year-old at one time." Did she just call me stupid? "You bring yourself over here tomorrow morning and we'll talk. So help me, Goddess, don't make me have to beat your ass, Siren." I smirked.

My mom was fifty-six years old, 5'2, and slim. She knew good and well her old ass wasn't beating MY big ass. Suddenly, I felt a hard pinch on my ear.

"Ouch!" I yelled.

"Don't play with me, girl," my mother said. I smiled because this lady was crazy.

"Love you, Ma. I'll see you tomorrow morning."

"Love you too, baby. Get some sleep."

Hanging up, I grabbed the broom to sweep up the glass and decided to open the window to let some of the nighttime breeze in. I dropped the broom when the breeze carried in a peculiar scent. Walking through the glass, not caring about the cuts the shards left on my feet since they would heal in minutes, I stepped as close to the window as I could get and inhaled. It was definitely a shifter, but not one of the regular shifters' scent I picked up on here and there. I never smelled a shifter's scent this close to my building. This one was strong, and I could tell it was male from the traces of the Creed cologne I picked up in it. It surrounded the building, as if he had done a full lap around the outside.

Quickly, I slammed the window shut and sprayed my lemon-scented air freshener all around the apartment like a mad woman. My gut was telling me some shit was about to go down sooner or later. I could literally smell it in the air. I did a quick protection spell so that no one could enter my home and headed to the bedroom. Fuck that glass and the rest of them dishes. I'd do them tomorrow.

5

DAME

"Look, all of that woofin' like you 'bout that shit, Betta stop that shit. Bitch I got something to make you lay down. Murder murder murder kill kill..."

I rapped along to that Omb Peezy, pushing my black Lexus coupe up to seventy miles per hour. So yeah, I'm Damian Black of the Black cartel, also known as Baby Black being that I'm the youngest. I know you already heard from Siren that I'm that nigga, but let me really introduce myself. I'm the muscle behind the cartel that consists of my four older brothers and numerous goons. I'm the nigga that'll walk up in your crib at three in the morning and pop your wife, your son, your daughter, and then finally you after I made you watch. Then, I'll head to IHOP and have breakfast like I hadn't killed an entire family moments before. I was one of those kids that watched horror movies back to back, then went to torture stray animals. My mother died giving birth to me, so I guess you could say she was my first murder. I'd been fucked up ever since.

Now, at the age of twenty-three, I had over two hundred bodies on my hands. A nigga wasn't completely heartless; I had remorse for a few. Mostly the kids and old people, but niggas knew what it was once you crossed the Black cartel or anybody we cared about. No one was safe. It didn't matter. I would see them niggas in hell when I made it there. Over the past couple of years, our empire expanded like crazy. It was all because of Siren's fine ass. She was the truth when it came to helping us out. A nigga like me ain't never believe in no afterlife, witches, fairies and goblins and shit. But goddamn, after dealing with her, I knew all that shit possible. I didn't go around broadcasting the shit because niggas would think I'd been fucking with that dust. Next thing you know, a nigga was trying you.

I pulled up to the abandoned warehouse in the middle of nowhere and cut the engine. I peeped two trucks belonging to Marsean and Troy, two of my brothers. Marsean and I were the closest since we were the closest in age. He was only a year older than me, but we could pass for twins, except he was lighter in complexion. Next was Amauri. He was twenty-seven and smart as fuck. I mean, the nigga went to college and everything. Hey, he made more money hustling than he would being a lawyer. Then there was Troy. Troy was thirty, and the only one of us married with kids. He normally didn't get involved with the bloody part of the business, which is why I was a little surprised to see his truck parked. Finally, there was Malachi, the oldest at thirty-four. This nigga swore he was our dad. Me and him bumped heads constantly. I mean, I loved the nigga and would take a bullet or shoot one for him, but he got on my nerves with all that fatherly behavior. He made it a point to call me reckless every fuckin' day. I mean, I could have been eating popcorn while watching TV, and this nigga would complain about that I was eating popcorn too reckless; that's how annoying he was with it. I wished that nigga would go 'head and have a kid or something so he could stop acting like I was his son. Back to the matter at hand. I popped my trunk and grabbed my black duffel bag, then headed inside the warehouse. Marsean was the first person I spotted leaned against the wall smoking a cigarette.

"What's up, bro?" he asked giving me dap.

"Ain't shit, my nigga," I responded.

"Niggas been waiting over an hour, fuck took you so long?" he questioned.

"Had something to handle."

He eyed me for a minute. "Only time you late is when you with Siren. So, I guess you was busy NOT getting pussy!" He chuckled at his own joke. I ain't find that shit funny.

"Fuck you." I spat, walking away and shaking my head.

Siren was my main bitch. I had other bitches that I fucked daily, but I wanted to fuck Siren. Even if I could fuck Siren, I would probably still fuck a few other chicks too. It would just be a lot less. What can I say? I loved pussy. I just wish there was a way to do it without her knowing. I loved Siren and didn't regret it, regardless of what she thought, but I loved pussy too. I saw how hurt she was when I fucked other bitches and sometimes, I contemplated just letting her go. Then, I got images of her wrapping her soft lips around another nigga like how she does to me, and a nigga got hot at the thought. I would kill that nigga and her ass too. So, letting her go wasn't even an option. I know you probably think I'm a selfish bastard.

"'Bout time, nigga," Troy said, glancing back at me.

His white wife beater was bloody. I ignored him 'cause I was tired of these motherfuckers thinking I had to explain myself to them. Looking around him, my eyes landed on a familiar face Well, what I could make out over the swelling looked familiar anyway.

"What happened?" I asked, facing Troy.

"Some money went missing on this nigga's watch. Nigga think I'm sweet after I put him on," Troy explained while taking a swig from his water bottle.

That's when it hit me. "Ain't this Tonya's brother?" I asked Troy.

He nodded. I shrugged. If he could deal with killing his wife's brother, then the shit damn sure didn't bother me.

"Man, please! Come on! We family!" The soon to be victim pleaded from his position tied to a chair.

I shook my head. "You ain't no kin to me."

Dropping my duffel bag, I squatted down and began rummaging through it until I found what I was looking for. I produced a handful of rusty nails and a hammer.

"Who got our cash?" I asked calmly.

"I don't know! I didn't have nothing to do with it! I did my job and went home!"

I nodded my head as if I believed him.

"Troy, take his shoes off."

Troy glanced at me. "What, you tryna make the nigga comfortable?"

When I didn't respond, he shook his head and took his brother in law's shoes off. "I ain't touchin' the nigga socks!" Troy said.

I chuckled "Alright, the socks can stay."

I placed one of the rusty nails over top of his big toe and brought my hammer down quick. I was Thor out this bitch right now.

"Ahhhhhhhhh!" He yelled.

"Who got our cash?" I asked once again.

This crying ass nigga was still begging and pleading for me to stop, but never answered my question. So, I grabbed another nail, placed it on top of the next toe and brought my hammer down again. I didn't even bother to ask another question before I grabbed another nail.

"Wait!!!" he screamed. I paused, holding my hammer in the air.

He was stuttering and mumbling, so I screamed, "Speak up, nigga!"

"Bear! This dude named Bear! He planning to have every one of the trap houses robbed!" he sobbed.

I turned to Troy, silently asking him if he knew this 'Bear' person. He shook his head. Kneeling down so I was eye level, being careful to avoid the blood seeping from his sock, I spoke. "Why did he feel comfortable enough with you to tell you the plan?"

"I... I don't know," he whispered. I could tell he was close to passing out so out of the kindness of my heart, I decided to help him out.

Swiftly, I brought the nail up to his face and hammered the nail into his eye. He screamed until he was hoarse, then he passed out. I glanced down. Fuck, some of that shit splashed on my shirt. Straightening up, I looked at Troy and Marsean, who decided to joined us.

"I'm not killing him just yet. I wanna know why that nigga felt cool enough to deal with him. He knows more," I said.

They each nodded. I packed up my bag, gave them dap, and headed out. My adrenaline was spiked, and I wanted to fall in some pussy before I went to sleep. It was damn near three in the morning. Sitting in my coupe, I scrolled through my phone, landing on this bitch Kayla I fucked from time to time. I decided to shoot her a text.

Me: you up?

Kayla: yes

Me: I'm coming over.

Kayla: ok daddy.

Tossing the phone on the passenger seat, I pulled off.

KAYLA WAS THIS THICK, red bone bitch whose pussy I was currently knee-deep in. She was face down, ass up on her bed, bouncing her fat ass all over my dick. I grabbed her blonde weave with both hand for leverage as I prepared to go deeper.

"Unnhhh! Oh my God! Yesssss!" She screamed.

I gripped her harder as she tried to climb away from me. "Stop running from the dick!" I yelled at her while pile driving into her.

She was screaming so loud, I mushed her head down into the bed to shut her up before she woke up her bad ass kids. She started squirming and ended up creaming all over the condom. Finally, I came. Sliding out of her, I headed to the bathroom to flush the condom.

"Are you staying the night?" she asked as I walked out of the bathroom.

"Do I ever stay the night?" I replied while getting dressed.

"No, but I mean, we been talking for a minute now, so—" I cut her ass off.

"We don't talk. We fuck." Snatching my phone and keys off the dresser, I headed toward the door.

I drove past Siren's crib before I headed home, something I

always did before I went home at night. If I didn't stay the night, I always checked on her. See? A nigga cared. Just had my own way of showing it. As I was about to pull off, something caught the corner of my eye. If I wasn't tripping, it was a big ass black and brown wolf coming out of the woods behind the building. I glanced at the blunt between my fingers and back at the huge wolf. Nah, I wasn't trippin', that was a fucking wolf. When it stood on two legs, it became damn near eye level with a second-floor window. What the hell? How is there big ass shit like this running around out here? This had to be one of them shifting motherfuckers Siren had told me about. I watched as it sniffed the ground and then the air, almost like it was searching for something it couldn't find. Even though my tinted windows were rolled up, I still heard the low growl it let out before hopping up into a tree and heading back into the woods, using tree tops as steps. I sat there for a few more moments to make sure that it didn't come back. Once I felt it wouldn't be back, I pulled off and made a mental note to have my weapons guy get me some silver bullets.

6

SIREN

I was up and dressed in a red maxi dress that clung to my curves and some gold strappy sandals. Last night had me a little worried and freaked out, so I made sure to lather myself in my peach grapefruit body butter, and then topped it off by rubbing myself down in Florida water. If you don't know about Florida water, Google is your friend. I wasn't about to get caught slipping out here with what I witnessed last night. I tossed the bottle of it into my over-sized tan purse, along with my wallet and key to my truck. As I walked down the stairs, I subtly sniffed, trying to see if I could smell the shifter from last night, but all I smelled was piss. When I stepped outside, I could smell all of him. The smell of him was in the air, but it was a lot lighter. Nowhere near as strong as last night. Glancing around, I saw a few of the regular dope boys who nodded when they spotted me. They never held their stare for too long because of the fear Dame instilled into them. I hit them with the head nod and looked to my right to see Drew, the tree climber, sitting on a crate, staring intently at his phone.

"Hey Drew," I said, making my way over to him.

He stared around nervously before putting his phone away.

"Hey, Siren. What's up beautiful?"

I eyed him for a minute; seeing how jumpy he was raised my suspicion. I didn't know if he didn't want word to travel to Dame that he had been spotted talking to me, or if it was something else. I touched his shoulder, trying to read his thoughts. Fear. He felt fear and as I tried to read deeper, he blocked me. Most humans didn't know how to block their thoughts unless they were those third eye, open chakra, meditating folk. Now, maybe I was being judgmental, but Drew didn't strike me as that type of person. I sniffed around him, just to be sure but I didn't smell anything out of the ordinary, just some tangerine. My eyes got a little bigger. Was he trying to cover a scent?

"What you wearing, Drew? You smell good," I told him, leaning a little closer to his neck.

He stood up. "Uhh, you know, I just grabbed some of my cousin's lotion out the bathroom this morning so a nigga wouldn't be ashy. You know that fruity shit y'all girls be wearing," he said, now sniffing me.

Taking a step back, I raised an eyebrow and stared at him. My gut feeling was that he was lying.

"Un huh," I said. "Let me ask you something... have you seen any new niggas around here?"

He cocked his head at me. "Nah. Why?"

I shrugged, ignoring his question. "Where you from, Drew?"

"Green River. Across the woods, but I'm staying with my cousin, Simone, just helping her out. She having baby daddy issues, you know what I mean? Nigga put his hands on her. So, I'll be here for a while."

I nodded, remembering the gossip Gee had told me about Simone. His story sounded good, but I was gonna definitely keep an eye on him.

"Yea, I feel you. Alright, Imma let you go, I gotta get going," I said, giving him a little wave as I walked off. Looking back, I caught him staring at my ass and he quickly turned his head. Chuckling to myself, I hopped in my truck and slowly pulled off.

~

I STOPPED at the grocery store to grab my mother's favorite chocolate croissants in an attempt to butter her up. The smell of rotting earth pierced my nostrils as I walked through the automatic doors. Vamps. Now, the description *'rotting earth'* may make you think of an unpleasant odor, but it actually wasn't. Imagine going to a forest the day after a hard rainstorm. Now, smell the dirt. That's similar to a vamp. I spotted her before she spotted me. She was tall, about my height, and caramel-skinned with long, straight hair. She wore extremely dark Versace shades inside the store. In her cart were gallons of orange juice. Vamps drank orange juice as a substitute for blood when they couldn't get the real thing. Something about the texture reminded them of human blood. She turned since she probably felt me coming because I never bothered to cloak my witch aura. She lifted her shades and looked me up and down with her violet eyes. I smiled and nodded. You know when you see another cute woman, and you acknowledge her because we too cute to hate on women empowerment. This bitch turned her nose up and turned her back. Vamps were so stuck up. Like bitch, you going to be bougie with your cold and dead ass pussy? Really?

Other witches would speak and be polite; hell, the aliens would talk your head off, asking you about this or that like they were tourists, but they were sweet. But these fucking vamps? Tuh. I bumped the shit out of her as I slowly walked past and looked at her, daring her to do something. She hissed lowly and bared her fangs. I pointed at her orange juice cartons and they exploded in her cart. Rolling my eyes, I kept it moving, making my way to the bakery section.

The loudspeaker blared, "Clean-up on aisle two!" as I perused the goodies until I found what I was looking for.

After paying for the desserts, I was once again on my way to my mother's house. My ringing phone interrupted the music blaring from the radio. *'Daddy'* flashed across the screen.

"Hey, Dame. What's up, baby?" I answered the phone.

"WHAT THE FUCK IS YOUR PROBLEM!?" he roared through my speakers.

I sighed. "What the fuck are you talking about now?"

"My homie said he saw you outside hollering at some nigga. He said you was all bent over in front of him and shit!" Damian continued to yell. I laughed loudly.

"First of all, your gossiping ass homie is exaggerating. Wasn't nobody bent over. I was just asking him if he noticed anything strange going on around the building, because after you left last night, I just had a weird feeling... and, I thought I heard some noise. Like howls that sounded close by."

"Oh shit! Listen, after I dealt with some business last night, I rode down your block just to check on things, and this big ass wolf came out those woods sniffing around the building. After a few minutes, it hopped up in the trees and disappeared back wherever it came from. You stay your ass out of them woods. Are you carrying the gun I got you?"

My heart sped up.

I just knew this shifter was looking for me, I could feel it in my gut. *Fuck fuck fuck!*

"Siren!" he yelled, bring me back to reality.

"N-no. It's in the house."

"My nigga," he said, taking a frustrated breath, "What the fuck good is it gonna do you in the crib and you outside?" Dame asked.

I never carried it because I didn't need it. I was my own weapon and could handle anything that came my way. Even I couldn't front; this shifter that was sniffing for me had me all kinds of scared.

"Listen, my mans is getting his hands on some silver bullets for me. I'm going to get some for you too. So, start carrying the gun," he made it a point to mention, again. At the mention of silver, I began to scratch my neck and chest. No, I would not be keeping any silver at my house. But I wasn't gonna tell him that.

"Ok," I whispered.

～

LOOKING BOTH WAYS, I crossed the street and gazed up at my mother's huge estate. Yes, I said estate. Home girl's neighbor was half a mile down the road. I adored her opulent grass, exotic flowers and trees, and the little coy fish pond that sat off to the side. What the untrained eye couldn't see was the invisible force field made with brick dust around the perimeter of her entire property, with tiny symbols drawn in it to keep out anyone who meant her harm and Jehovah's witnesses. Carefully, I stepped over it so I didn't disturb her spell and walked up her circular driveway. Before I could knock, the door swung open. My mother was a beautiful and petite woman. Her caramel skin and youthful face always glowed like a teenager. She had long, thick hair that was shiny and curled in loose waves. She wore a pantsuit because she always meant business. The only thing that took away from her professional business look were the rings that she wore on each of her fingers.

My mother had a ring for every finger with earth stones, from turquoise to tiger's eye. The frankincense fragrance she always wore brought back fond memories of my childhood.

"Well, baby girl, we have a lot to talk about." She was staring at me with her large, slanted and reddish-brown eyes that were a replica of my own. Smiling, she wrapped me in a tight hug before pulling me into her huge home with the high ceilings. Of course, before I could even sit my purse down, she started in on me.

"Have you had sex?"

"Ma!" I yelled, spinning around to face her.

She waved me off. "Oh, child please. You've always been hot in the ass. I remember when—"

"I brought you croissants," I said, handing her the peace offering I had brought.

Placing her hands on her hips, she smirked, "Nice try." Still didn't stop her from snatching the box out of my hands. Now that she was busy digging into her favorite dessert, it was my turn to get sassy.

"Besides ma, you had sex. So, why can't I? It's not fair!" I yelled, throwing a tantrum like a giant child. I even stomped my foot for good measure.

"Get your ass in the kitchen and sit down," she said, licking chocolate off her fingers.

Sighing loudly, I strolled to the kitchen and placed my bag on the round, glass table before pulling out my chair. My mother walked in behind me and stared me up and down, trying to tell if I had done the deed or not.

"Pour us some tea," she told me. I was about to stand and head to the cupboard for tea cups, but she pushed me back down. I looked at her confused.

"Do it from here," she demanded.

"Seriously, ma?" I sucked my teeth.

She was silent, watching and waiting. Lifting my finger, I used my magic to open the cupboard and float the blue and white China teacups over to the table. Then, I pointed at the tea kettle on the stove and flew it over to carefully pour the hot tea. And, because I wanted to show off, I pointed to the window, which faced her back-yard garden. It opened. She looked at me questioningly while I smirked and played with my nails. A honey comb glided through the open window and poured a few drops of honey in each cup, then I sent it back out the window. Lightly, I blew in each cup and formed small tornadoes to stir in the honey. When I was done, I snapped my fingers and everything ceased. Grabbing my cup, making sure my pinky finger was up, I took a small sip. Finally, I looked up at my mother, who was still standing there, shocked. She burst out laughing and soon, I was too.

"You little bratty show off!" she said in between laughter.

"At least you know I didn't have sex now," I whimpered.

Pulling out a seat, she sat down and brushed imaginary lint off her pants. She cleared her throat before she spoke.

"I was twenty-three, when I met your father. He was tall, dark, and handsome and the moment our eyes connected, I knew he was somebody special. I was scared to get too close to him because... well. You know. The rule." I nodded, waiting for her to continue. "But eventually, he wore me down and I went on a date with him. We dated for months before the topic of sex came up. I told him what was up, and he was so understanding. I didn't get any argument from him at all, and we continued to date like nothing had changed. It was a year later when he asked me to marry him. By now, I knew he was a shifter and would be breaking major laws in his community by marrying outside of his species. He didn't care. He didn't care about the laws, he didn't care that we couldn't be intimate, he just wanted me. He was willing to give up everything just to be with me," she spoke, wiping a stray tear.

"So, you know what? I decided to give up something too. We were intimate for the first time ever and within minutes, my magic was gone. The love I had for your father, and then your brother, and then you filled the void when my magic left. It took years for me to relearn simple spells. You've watched me struggle over the years. I'm just now getting some of my natural magic back."

To demonstrate, she pointed at the tea kettle on the table, and it lifted slowly and shakily into the air. I could see her struggling to fly it back to the stove top. It was almost there and then, it fell from the air. I caught it with my magic right before it hit the floor. Gently, I placed it on the stove.

"I would do the same thing all over again," she said about my father. "I say this to you to say, make sure it's worth it." Damn. I really had some shit to think about now. "Now, tell me about why you killed that girl?" I put my head down and looked up at her with guilty eyes.

"She told me she was fuc— um... having relations with Dame." My mother shook her head, disappointed.

"What type of man would even put you in that situation? And, this is the man you are willing to risk your magic for? Just tacky," she judged while shaking her head. Leave it to my mom to make sense and make me feel bad. I sat back and folded my arms.

"Fine, mom! I won't do it. Happy now?"

"Sure am." She ignored my attitude. "Now, tell me about the shifting last night."

I filled her in on most of the events from last night. She nodded as I spoke. "Hold on. I have something for you," she said, standing and walking out of the kitchen.

Maybe Dame and I weren't meant to be together. My father waited for my mother and didn't cheat with other women. Dame was known to mess with other females, so was he worth me losing my powers over? It had me questioning if Dame would be able to fill my void if I lost my magic, like my father did for my mother. Then again, me and my brother also filled the void, and me and Dame had no children and I wasn't planning on it.

"Here." my mother reappeared and handed me a thick, dusty book. The book looked ancient and very important. I blew the thick layer of dust off the cover and looked at the title. *SHIFTING FOR DUMMIES*. I looked at my mother.

"Really?" She held her hands up in surrender

"I didn't name the book." Tossing the book in my purse, I stood to leave.

"Siren, I want you to be careful. Your father came to me in a dream last night. He's trying to warn me about something... but I can't... I don't know what it is, but in my heart, I think it involves you." I nodded my head.

"I'll be careful, Mom. I promise." I promised her. We embraced before I left. Although she shed some light on what happened last night, I left her house more confused than when I arrived.

7

BEAR

I'm three-hundred years old, which is just a baby in shifter years. In human years, I was twenty-one years old. I've been the Alpha of the Green River pack for about fifty years, and my main goal in life was to get to the dollar. Everything was cool, until talk started circulating about the Black Cartel from Bellmont trying to take my shit over. Why didn't I just tear them limb from limb, right? I'm a shifter, after all. I have tried numerous times. It's like these niggas got some type of divine protection. Every single time I've tried to set them up, they somehow weren't where they were supposed to be. Every time I've tried to strike, someway, those niggas made it out. I sent one of my betas over there to check things out and see how they were operating. It was simple to get in one of their worker's ear. One night, I heard him bitching about the Black brothers and decided to make him an offer. It had been days, and I couldn't reach that nigga. He was probably caught slipping. Did it seem like I was worried? If you thought I was, you're a clown.

"Ahhhhhh, fuck. Take all this nut, bitch." I gripped the back of Maya's head as I fucked her face harder, causing her to gag.

I exploded down her throat and held her still so she would swallow everything. She sucked everything down, then wiped her mouth before walking out. I watched her leave and enjoyed the view of her plumped ass switching away. Damn, she just sucked the soul from me. Our women's jaws were strong as fuck. Catching my breath, I sat back, sparking my loud. Now, where was I? Oh yea, even though the one dude went missing, I still had my own man over there. My phone interrupted me from smoking this blunt and going through my thoughts.

"What's the word, my man?" I answered the phone.

"Not too much yet, but I know where Baby Black bitch ass lives. It's something about her though, man, I think she's a witch. The bitch read my mind, 'til I put up a block. I'm willing to bet she's the reason these niggas can't be touched. Something else... I think she might be a shifter too." Now, this was some shit.

"Drew, what the fuck you mean *you think*? Did you smell the bitch?!" I yelled, irritated.

"Nah, I can't pick up a scent from her, but I think she's covering it... she smelled Mega... I mean, I think she did. Man listen, I think we should hold off until Mega—"

I cut him right the fuck off because I knew where his scary ass was going. "Drew, don't call the fuck back 'til you got something I want to hear, real shit. And, as far as Mega goes, ain't nobody scared of that nigga!" I screamed, ending the call.

So, I guess I should explain who Mega's ass was. Every pack had their own Alpha, but all alphas answer to Mega. Mega is the alpha of all alphas, but this nigga only shows his face once every hundred years or so, to make sure everybody was following these ancient ass rules. I'm sure he was only sniffing around 'cause one of them Bellmont shifters mangled some bitch and left her in the woods for the humans to find. Mega was the one always talking about eat only when hungry and show respect and leave no remains. Blah, blah, blah. Listen, fuck Mega, old fake ass Idris Elba-looking nigga, and all these dumb ass rules. I'm the one out here in the trenches. Everybody feared this motherfucker. I was sick of bowing to him. All these niggas had me pissed the fuck off.

"MAYA! Get out here, I want some pussy!" I yelled, taking one more pull from my blunt before putting it out.

She slowly walked out with tears in her eyes, so I prepared myself for some more dumb shit. "You said if I sucked your dick, I wouldn't have to fuck you. You know I'm supposed to be mated with Drew. You're already mated..."

Before she could finish, I backhanded her and she flew into the wall, dropping to the ground.

"Bitch, I'm the alpha! You should feel fucking privileged that I wanna stick my dick in you, are you crazy?" I roared at her. She balled up on the floor and sobbed. "You know what? Bitch, I don't even wanna fuck you no more. You're disgusting. Imma go home and fuck your sister," I told her as I walked out and slammed the door behind me. I was mated to her sister anyway, fuck that hoe. A bitch was crazy if she thought I had a shortage of pussy.

8
———

DAME

I was ready to nut the fuck up when my young bull hit me talking about my bitch was outside in broad daylight, having a conversation and parading around in front of some new nigga. Just thinking about it again caused my blood to boil. That shit was disrespectful. I told my little niggas to find out everything they could about that nigga. Little did he know, he was more than likely living in his last days. It would be smart for him to head back to wherever the fuck he came from. Then, this bitch Kayla keep blowing my phone up, talking about she was pregnant. I told her ass I used condoms, so it wasn't mine. She already had four kids, so you would think her trifling ass would be on birth control or some shit. I had been in the warehouse torturing this nigga for days now. Most of his body looked like an open wound. I had this torture shit down to a science. I knew how to miss all the vital organs and do just enough to inflict maximum pain without killing a nigga. I had one of them long ass white aprons on since I had started skinning dude. I didn't wanna mess up my True Religion jeans, you feel me?

"Please, just kill me," he whispered. Sweat and blood mixed all over his face, he had the shakes and dry heaves. The smell in here was rancid as fuck too, probably because he had been going to the bathroom on himself.

I should have had one of those surgical masks for this shit. I was ready to kill his ass and get this shit over with.

"Nah, I ain't doing you no favors until you do one for me. Tell me what I want to know," I decided to bargain with him while wiping his blood off my machete with the white apron, leaving a smeared crimson stain. The shit was my favorite color.

Slowly, he nodded. "Bear, he's from Green River," That caused me to raise my brow. I knew that was why Malachi wanted to have the meeting tomorrow night. The takeover of Green River.

"Yeah? Keep talking."

"I was out at the bar, the day Troy spazzed out on me at the house. Nigga called me a fuck-up. I was drunk, talking shit about him to anybody that would listen. Bear walked up and offered me a spot in his organization if I helped him take out y'all trap houses." My jaw was tight.

This ungrateful ass motherfucker was struggling to feed his family before Troy put him on. Now, this nigga had a nice crib, fly wheel, and his shorty was never hungry.

"Just one thing, man, just make sure my daughter straight? She and her mother ain't have nothing to do with this."

I nodded my head. His daughter would be straight, only 'cause she was kin to Troy's wife. "Can I have some water?" he whispered.

He was going too far, playing on my good nature. I shook my head. "Nigga, you was thirsty in life, stay thirsty in death." I told him before I plunged the machete straight into his throat. I twisted it before I snatched it out, leaving a gaping hole clear through his neck.

He only had one eye since the other was removed after I plunged a nail into it, and that one eye bulged as he struggled to breathe. He twitched for three seconds before finally dying. I could have just gave him a head shot to make that shit quick, but I still wanted him to suffer. I didn't appreciate him out talking shit about Troy.

"Nigga, never bite the hand that feeds you," I said to his body, hoping he heard me from wherever he was now.

Untying the apron, I placed it on the small table next to the chair this fuck nigga's body was slumped in and grabbed my phone out of my pocket. After powering it on, I placed a call to the cleanup crew, hopped in my red Benz, and sped off. Before I could even make it up the road, my phone went off. Breathing heavily after seeing Kayla's name flash across my phone, I answered and snapped.

"Bitch, stop calling me. I used condoms. I'm trying not to kill your ass." I could hear her crying.

"Not every time we used condoms, Damian. Why you doing this?! For that bitch Si—" I cut her off.

"Don't say her fucking name, bitch. Now, get off my line and go find your baby daddy, 'cause it ain't me." I hung up and threw the phone on my passenger seat.

Truth was, there was a possibility that her baby could be mine. I had a couple drunk nights where I ran in these bitches raw. Each time I pulled out, but we know that didn't mean shit. Sperm would still fight to get into a bitch's pussy, and that's how babies were made. A nigga was praying that this baby wasn't mine. If Siren found out, she would be done with my ass for good and I couldn't take that. My phone started ringing again, which further irritated me.

"WHAT!!!!" I roared without even checking to see who was calling.

"Nigga, what the fuck is wrong with you?" My oldest brother, Malachi, yelled through the line.

"Man, that bitch Kayla keep calling talking 'bout she pregnant and shit," I explained my frustration with him.

"Nigga! I told you about being reckless out here. Now, you 'gon have to deal with that slimy bitch."

"I'm not for this shit right now, bro."

"Nah, fuck that. You need to hear it. If that ghetto bird is pregnant, it's gonna get back to Siren. Bitches run off emotions and shit. Suppose she don't wanna work with us no more? You fucking up for everybody, little nigga," he spat. "Another house got hit today while you were auditioning for the Maury show. Did you find anything out?"

"What house?" I ignored his little Maury comment.

"Your house, nigga. Where the fuck yo' niggas at?"

"FUCK!" I barked before hanging up and heading over that way.

I PULLED up in front of Siren's building to check the little niggas out here. They were supposed to be in charge of my trap house and the shit was ghost town, which was rare for it to be three in the afternoon. Quickly mixing some sprite with some cough syrup, I tossed it back and stepped out my whip. I walked in Siren's building, but instead of going to the fourth floor that she was on, I went to the second to see about my trap. Pulling out my hammer, I walked in with murder on my mind. Marsean was already here questioning two of the little niggas that worked for us. I looked around, until my eyes landed on my open and now emptied safe. Then, I scanned over the two niggas that sat quiet watching me.

"What the fuck happened?" I asked quietly while rubbing my temple with the gun.

"Man, this big nigga ran up in here telling us to come up off the cash. We started bustin' at 'im, but... it was like the shots wasn't even affecting him! I know we hit 'im! I ain't never seen no shit like that in my life!"

"Nigga crushed our guns and knocked us out! When we came to, the safe was empty. I called you, but your phone was off, so then I called Malachi," the other one chimed in. I stared at them for a minute before looking around. I counted at least eight bullet holes in the wall, but no blood.

I looked at Marsean, who gave me the same bewildered look. "Let me see your guns," I said.

They each pulled out mangled pieces of metal that looked like they used to be guns.

"Wait... where the fuck is Jordan?" I asked. Jordan was the one who told me about Siren the other day, and also the nigga I put in charge of this house.

"We can't find him. His baby mom ain't even seen him."

I was getting frustrated. "What this hulk nigga look like?" I asked. The youngest one spoke up.

"Like a big strong ass Al. B Sure-looking nigga. Curly hair and everything."

I would've laughed if there wasn't so much shit going on right now.

I nodded my head and pointed my thumb over my shoulder.

"Y'all can go, but I wanna hear something about Jordan." They nodded and practically ran out the door. "And, keep this to yourselves!" I yelled before they could get all the way out.

Putting my gun back in my waist, I ran my hands over my head.

"You think it was a shifter?" Marsean asked.

I nodded my head. "Had to be." Nobody else could've taken them shots, mangled metal guns, knocked out two street niggas, and still hit the safe."

I filled him in on everything that Troy's brother in law told me. "Go tell the others. I can't be around Malachi right now. I'm gonna clear my head and get up with y'all tonight," I told him.

"Be safe, bro," he warned me before giving me dap and heading out.

I sat on the old sofa that was in the room and tried to piece everything together. Everything kept coming back to this nigga, Bear. If this was Bear that came up in here today, I knew I would need those silver bullets sooner rather than later. I could feel the loud and lean starting to kick in, so I left out and jogged up the two flights of stairs to get to Siren's crib. I wanted some pussy, but I would settle for some of her bomb ass head. I was starting to feel a little woozy by the time I banged on her door. She opened the door, looking good as ever, wearing some black tights and one of them cut off t-shirts that stop right under her breasts. If she raised her arms, the bottoms of her round tits would be visible.

"Congratulations," she said blandly, causing me to finally look up at her face.

She didn't look happy to see a nigga. I leaned in to try and kiss her, but she turned her head. Today had to be national piss Dame off day.

"What's your problem?" I grilled her.

She looked at me like she was disgusted before shoving her phone at me. This bitch was like two seconds from getting slapped. I had never put my hands on her, besides gripping her up from time to time, but her level of disrespect right now was crazy to me. I shot her a look to let her know she was on thin ice before I stared down at her phone. It took me a minute to realize what I was looking at.

"Fuck!" I yelled, looking at Kayla's Instagram page, where she'd posted a picture of a sonogram. I scrolled down to read the caption.

I'm gonna be a mommy again. @sirenfalls I'll let Dame know what I need so you can bring it to the baby shower, step mommy! Muah!'

The pic had about hundred likes and two-hundred comments. People were saying everything from congratulations, to calling her foul bitches, to just laughing. Siren's face was a mask of anger as she glared at me. Damn, I felt like shit. I couldn't think of anything to say except what I been saying to Kayla's ass.

"It ain't mine." The last thing I remember before she closed the door in my face was the hurt in her eyes.

9

SIREN

"Ouch, not so tight with my edges!" I yelled.

This was why I hated coming to the shop to get my dreads re-twisted. Bitches loved to play tug of war with my edges. I'd be damned if they had me walking around looking like a radish. Normally, I would do it myself at home, but I needed a little pampering. Bet you thought I would start this chapter whining and crying about Damian, didn't you? After some serious soul-searching, self-control and fifteen-hundred dollars' worth of damages to my apartment last night, I decided I was done with Damian Black and the Black Cartel. After tonight, I was no longer going to continue to help them take over everything. What you thought? I wasn't going to go to that meeting tonight and get my final five figure payment? I planned to go dressed up and looking better so Dame's ass would be drooling. I also made up my mind that I was going to move out of the projects. Gee and I were going house hunting soon. She came over last night, armed with snacks and her Netflix password because that's what sisters do. We alternated between movies, talking shit, and stalking that hoe Kayla's social media pages.

"You done," the pretty, but heavy handed Jamaican woman told me. She patted me on my shoulder.

"Yaassss!" I yelled while looking in the mirror. Home girl had styled the top part of my hair in the shape of a small crown and adorned it with gold cuffs, while the back half hung down to my butt crack in big twists. Even my baby hair was in formation. I felt like a million bucks in my short green tunic dress and sandals that strapped all the way up to my thighs.

After tipping her heavily, I walked out and enjoyed the stares and compliments that were being tossed my way. The breeze felt so good on my scalp that I slowed my walk, just enjoying the fresh air. Sniffing, I stopped in my tracks. The familiar smell of the shifter that was creeping around my building surrounded me. I even smelled the Creed Cologne mixed in. He was close. Real close. Casually, I looked around, not wanting to blow my cover. It was a nice day out, so there was a pile of people out walking around on both sides of the street. I knew I should have just slid into my truck and took my ass home, but I needed to see him. I can't lie, his smell was intoxicating. It was different from the other shifters. There was no hiding the fact that I was turned on. I decided not to wear a bra today, and my nipples were suddenly hard as rocks.

I dropped my purse as the bones in my hand started snapping. Glancing down, I watched my nails transform into sharp red claws before my eyes. Quickly, I dropped down, gathering the contents that spilled out of my bag. I stayed down there, pretending to be searching for something, but I was doing every mental technique I could think of to stop myself from shifting. A tear rolled down my eye as I felt my hand slowly returning to normal. Breathing a sigh of relief, I inhaled his scent. It felt as though I was floating in it.

"Need some help?" a deep voice questioned me. I was paralyzed.

After I just talked all that shit about wanting to see what he looked like, here he was, directly in front of me and I was terrified to look up. Fuck, curiosity killed the cat. His voice sounded almost musical. I could hear a very slight accent, but I couldn't place from where. Instead of answering him or looking up, I stared at his black Dolce and Gabanna sneakers. I didn't know why I thought I was on Jurassic park and if I didn't move, maybe he wouldn't see me. Reaching down, he gently pulled me up. His touch felt familiar, but still managed to send chills down my spine. I took the quick opportunity to scan his thoughts to see if he meant me any harm. Affection, caring, love, and protection ran through his mind clearly. Lastly was lust, but I could tell he struggled with that one. Suddenly, I was blocked. He blocked me. I looked up and smirked. Lord, why did I look up? I was staring straight at Stringer Bell from that HBO series *the wire*. Yup, I was looking at a young Idris Elba. He was facing the sun, and the light shone all over his flawless and dark chocolate skin. He had the type of skin that looked like his mama used to slather cocoa butter all over it. Like, I'm a hundred percent sure he used to be one of those little greasy faced kids you see running around the neighborhood.

His eyes were the color of warm coffee and when he smiled, he revealed a set of perfectly white teeth, framed by full, soft-looking lips and a precision-cut goatee. His hair was thick and shiny and filled with waves. Those perfect waves that a surfer would hang ten on are always on a quest to find. Towering over me, I guesstimated he had to be at least 6'5 or 6'6. The simple gray fitted Polo tee and distressed jeans he wore did nothing to hide his muscular physique. Tribal tattoos ran up both his toned arms and around his neck. And, oh my gods, you already knew about the scent. My senses were in overdrive. All of them. I didn't even notice I was biting my bottom lip, imagining all the nasty things I wanted to do to his dick. Speaking of, this man was too perfect. Doesn't that usually mean they had a little dick or erectile dysfunction or some shit? But he was a shifter, so I knew he had a big dick.

"It's not polite to read people's thoughts," he whispered to me in a low growl. He leaned close to my ear as he whispered into it. I tilted my head up so I could feel his breath on my neck. Chills shot straight from my neck, down to my pussy. Damn, I think I just came a little.

"I had to make sure I wasn't in danger." I breathed with my eyes closed, still trying to recover from my mini orgasm.

"You're never in danger when I'm around," he assured me with his voice vibrating through my body.

Opening my eyes, they connected with his. I believed him. He was so close that I could kiss him. I actually contemplated doing just that, but my shoulder snapped. Gasping, I backed up and covered my shoulder with my hand. When he noticed what was happening, he moved swiftly to shield my body with his, wrapping his arm around my waist and blocking me from onlookers. To anyone walking past, we just looked like two young lovers having a PDA moment.

"You don't know how to control it?" he asked.

I shook my head. I had so many questions, like, how does he know what I am? Can he smell me through the citrus? Why wasn't he trying to kill me? And, why the hell did I feel so comfortable around him?

"It's only recently been like this. It started a few nights ago, but then I was fine until today. It has happened twice today," I blurted, breaking out into a sweat from struggling to keep from shifting.

Suddenly, I knew what was happening. I saw the exact moment when the light came on in his mind, realizing what was going on. He quickly backed up off me and looked around nervously. Clearing his throat, he stooped down to gather my things that fell from my purse.

Once he handed me the bag, I replied. "I umm... I should go." He was silent as he walked me the rest of the way to my truck.

He opened the door so I could climb in. It seemed like we were both waiting for something as I sat in the driver's seat. I made no movement to put the key in the ignition, and he hadn't closed the door yet. Instead, he stood there with both hands placed firmly on the roof of the car, watching me.

"By the way, I read your thoughts too and it didn't seem like you were worried that you were in danger," he smirked with a cocky smile.

Oh hell no. Without hesitation, I put up a block on this nigga. He laughed. "Wait. Shifters can't read minds," I said.

He had to be fucking with me. "I'm a different breed, Siren." he replied.

Dammit! So now, this nigga knew I had an orgasm in the middle of the sidewalk. I could feel my face heating up as I dropped my head. How embarrassing? I guess he sensed my humiliation because he placed a crooked finger under my chin and lifted my head. Shaking his head, he spoke.

"Don't be embarrassed. Even if I couldn't read your mind, I would've smelled you. Your scent drives me crazy." He lightly sniffed the air around me, causing me to clench my thighs together tightly.

"Why are you able to smell me through the citrus?" I asked.

"I already told you. I'm a different breed, Siren," he repeated, not really coming up off any information.

"You know my name, what's yours?" I asked.

"Mega."

I nodded my head, "Fitting," I said, causing him to smile.

"I'll see you around, Siren," he told me, and stepped back and closed my door.

I stopped him before he could close it all the way. "Not if I see you first, Mega." He grinned at me before he turned to walk away.

I probably would have sat in the same spot all day replaying everything that happened if my ringing phone wouldn't have pulled me kicking and screaming from my fantasies.

"Girl, where are you? You was supposed to have been here half hour ago!" Gianna yelled.

Shit! I totally forgot about us doing lunch today.

"Friend, I didn't realize it got so late. I'm on my way now, order for me!" I told her and ended our call. I looked around once more for Mega, but he was gone.

GEE DROPPED her fork onto the plate of chicken alfredo she was devouring moments before. It made a loud clinking noise as the silver hit the glass plate. It wasn't real silver or I would have been tearing this entire establishment up.

"WHAT!?" she yelled, causing other patrons inside of the *Ruby Tuesday's* to glance in our direction.

I looked around nervously while taking a sip of my red wine. "Gee, have a little class," I whispered across the table.

Her eyes ballooned. "Bitch, no you didn't!"

I doubled over in laughter.

"I'm glad you think the shit is funny. You were face to face with a shifter? A pure blood shifter. Probably the only reason he didn't kill you was because there were too many witnesses around." She rolled her eyes.

I shook my head and started to dig into my loaded mashed potatoes. "I read his thoughts, Gee. He cares for me. Besides, he's my mate," I nonchalantly replied.

"Your mate?" she asked, using air quotation marks. "Now you fluent in beast lingo," she cackled sarcastically.

I narrowed my eyes. I swear, sometimes I thought this bitch forgot I was part beast.

"Remember the book my mom gave me that I was telling you about?" She nodded. "Well, one thing it said was when young women are in the presence of their mate, their bodies will shift uncontrollably, until they master control or finally consummate with him. Now, because I'm a mixed breed, the rules aren't defined. Like, if I have sex with a shifter or male witch, my powers will remain intact. And, I know it's him. Every time my body has involuntary shifted, I've been sexually worked up and I've smelled his scent," I said, cutting into my steak.

Gee sucked her teeth. "Look, I get it. You're a twenty-five-year-old virgin. But, you can't be going around thinking with your hormones."

I choked on my wine and glanced around again. "Damn bitch, the whole restaurant don't have to know I'm a virgin," I whispered across the table.

"I'm sorry, but I'm grieving. My best friend's funeral will be held in a couple weeks," she said, dabbing imaginary tears from the corners of her eyes with a napkin.

I sucked my teeth at her dramatic ass. "Bitch, ain't nothing getting killed but this pussy."

"Excuse me, ladies, I overheard your conversation," a man said, looking at me. " I wanted to lend a little support. I'm thirty-two and I'm a proud virgin." I looked around again.

I couldn't believe all the L's I was taking today. "I teach an absti-nence class over at the youth center. I'd love for you to be a guest speaker one day. Remember, no sex is safe sex," he recited and placed his card on the table.

I stared down at his card. "Nah Jerry, not today, bruh," I said, flicking his card off the table. Gianna burst into a fit of giggles. Yeah, I was ready to go.

Outside, in the parking lot, we stopped short, noticing that Gee had a flat. Upon closer inspection, I noticed all four of her tires had been flattened.

"Okay, Bitch! Who's man you fuckin'?" I inquired, turning to face her.

Crossing her arms, she said, " Remember that dude, Rell, I met in front of your building? Well, we been kicking it since then, but he neglected to tell me he had a girl and a kid at home." She scowled. "So, she called my phone and I came at her, woman to woman." She paused, throwing a hand on her hip while I rolled my eyes, "And, told her that her no-good nigga was playing us both, but this bitch still wants to come at me," she explained, throwing her hands in the air.

I shook my head. All this drama over that little ass nigga.

"Well, call AAA and have it towed. In the meantime, just ride with me. I need to stop home." I told her.

We walked over to my truck while she spoke on her cell, giving AAA her location. As we walked, I smiled to myself, thinking about Mega. Out of habit, I sniffed the air, but all I smelled was cooked food from the restaurant and exhaust fumes. As we walked to my truck, my phone started to ring. I had an incoming call from a number that I failed to recognize. Sucking my teeth, I stared at the phone because I knew it was no one but Dame. Decline. He called and texted a million times last night, until I finally blocked his ass. I had to see him tonight at the meeting and then, he would see that I was seri-ously done with his ass. I wished I would shed another tear over his smut ass. Now that I thought about it, I needed to wear something fly as fuck tonight, so he could see what he was going to be missing. My petty meter was at an all-time high as we peeled out of the parking lot bumping Cardi B.

When we pulled up to my building, I was pissed to see some random nigga parked their blue BMW in my parking spot. I parked directly behind them, boxing them in so they'd have to find me when they were ready to leave. We both got out and looked around, trying to figure out whose car it could have been, but there was no one out. No dope boys, crack heads, bad ass kids, and no blaring car systems. Now that I thought about it, it had been dryer than brittle hair around here the past couple of days.

"Gee, what you know about the dry spell around here?" I asked action news. She shrugged.

"From what I hear, niggas is just poppin' up missing. But, it's only the d boys," she said.

As we walked inside my building, I was shocked to see my brother, Mike, posted on the step, playing on his phone.

"Mikey!" I screeched, running over to him. He smiled, showing his dimples as he stood.

"What's up, baby girl?" he asked, grabbing me into a tight hug and cutting off my air.

"Damn, nigga!" I said, struggling to escape his embrace. Mike was caramel-skinned, like our mother, but he stood 6'2. He was buff, and I guess he was cute. He never seemed to have a shortage of women. Of course, Gee was drooling all over herself, with her thirsty ass.

"Hey, Mike," she said in a flirty voice. I rolled my eyes as Mike focused in on her.

"What's up, Gee? Damn, you really grew up on a nigga, huh?" he said, eyeing her body.

Ok, this shit was gross. "What you doing slumming in the PJs?" I joked.

He ripped his eyes away from Gianna's body, and his face grew serious as he spoke.

"Ma told me about that fuck nigga you dealing with. I came over here to check on you and talk some sense into you."

I sighed because he thought he was my father. Placing a hand on my hip, I replied to him. "You're too late because I've already come to my senses, and I'm done with him."

"You fuckin' right you are!" he yelled, determined to have the last word– like always.

Ahh, the joy of a big brother. We walked up the four flights of stairs to my apartment, and I tried to keep my lunch down as Gee and Mike flirted. With every step we took, they had some little flirty words they shared between the both of them. Inside, they made themselves comfortable in the living room, while I jumped in the shower and changed into some sweats and a T-shirt to lounge around in until it was time to head out to the Black's meeting.

I already had my fit laid out, and it was going to bring Dame to his knees. That fucking clown just lost a real one. As I walked out of the bedroom, I heard the end of Gee's story.

"So, the guy gave her his business card and left. I just about died," she recapped what went on at lunch to my brother.

As I stepped into the room, they erupted in laughter. I mean, my brother was stomping his foot and trying to catch his breath from laughing so hard. This big nigga was knocking over my knick knacks and shit. I raced to my poor crystal elephant and caught it just before it hit the floor.

"Glad y'all think that shit is funny. Gee, why don't you get Mike to take you to pick up your car when AAA calls, since you two are so chummy," I said smartly.

"What happened to your car?" he asked her. She shot me a dirty look while I stuck my tongue out at her.

I went to the kitchen and grabbed a gallon of water, hopped up on my counter, and guzzled it. I looked outside my window and spotted three of the usual crack heads quickly walking down the block. Shit, finally some people outside. I was really starting to wonder what in the hell was going on in the neighborhood.

"Si, Gee's had a hard day. We're going to go out and get some drinks before she picks up her car," Mike informed me.

Raising a brow, I smirked. "Ummm hmmm. Sure." He gave me that same grin that reminded me of our childhood, when we would get our asses in trouble. "I'll call you later, and I meant what I said about that fuck nigga. Y'all are done," he decided to remind me for the second time, as if the first time wasn't enough.

As I walked him to the door, I could've sworn I already made that call, but I didn't feel like arguing so I simply nodded. He walked out with Gee following behind him, but she quickly stopped and faced me, sticking her tongue out. I chuckled and closed the door on her. That bitch was so childish. I would be the one laughing when they realized I had blocked Mike's car in.

10

DAME

"Fuck!" I barked as Siren declined another one of my calls from my burner phones.

I was sitting inside my brother, Marsean's, condo. He was the only person I felt comfortable enough with to tell him everything that went down last night. As far as this Bear nigga, I took it upon myself to replace the whole crew's guns with silver bullets. No one had seen him since he ran into my trap. I was ready to roll into Green River blasting, but something else that had popped on my radar; all my niggas were slowly disappearing. I had been driving past a few of my trap houses and where they usually looked like a club let out, there was now only a handful of niggas outside. On top of losing my bitch and my niggas, I was also losing money. I had enough bread stashed to afford myself the lifestyle I'd become accustomed to, but I knew it would only last me two to three years tops. I never invested in anything because I had planned on getting it forever. I made a mental note to talk to my brother, Amauri, about flipping this money to become legal. I needed to start moving smarter with my money; hell, with everything else too.

In the meantime, I planned to get back all the shit that I lost. I dialed Siren again, and she sent me straight to voicemail again. I ran my hands over my head and looked up at the ceiling. This shit was frustrating.

"Yo bro, you gotta shake this shit off. Come on, man," Marsean spoke.

I hadn't even realized he had walked into the living room. I nodded my head slowly. "I know," I responded. He eyed me for a moment.

"If I didn't know better, I'd think you were more torn over Siren than this cash, nigga."

I shook my head, "Nah. Never that," I told a boldfaced lie.

He continued to stare at me before plopping down on the lush loveseat across from me.

"Cool." He leaned up to the table, preparing to roll some loud. "So, what happened with the Kayla bitch earlier?" he asked, changing the subject.

My face immediately filled with anger at the thought of her. I had threatened her ass until she took down that nut ass post and forced her into another doctor's appointment, because I wanted to know exactly when her baby was conceived. I told that bitch if I found out she was lying, she and whoever's baby she was carrying were good as dead.

"We went to the doctor's office, and they said she was about five weeks and some days. Shit added up to the night we threw that party. I couldn't find Siren, so I left with Kayla. I was twisted," I told him, shaking my head.

"Damn, so it really is yours?" He ran the lighter up and down the blunt to dry it.

I shook my head. "I don't know. The doctor couldn't tell me the exact time. Shit, for all I know, that bitch could have fucked somebody else earlier in the day." Marsean paused as he was about to light his blunt.

"Nigga. You wild." He started cracking up laughing.

I had to laugh too, even though I was dead ass serious. I knew what type of bitch Kayla was. "Nigga, spark the weed so we can get to this fucking meeting," I demanded.

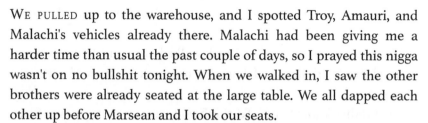

WE PULLED up to the warehouse, and I spotted Troy, Amauri, and Malachi's vehicles already there. Malachi had been giving me a harder time than usual the past couple of days, so I prayed this nigga wasn't on no bullshit tonight. When we walked in, I saw the other brothers were already seated at the large table. We all dapped each other up before Marsean and I took our seats.

"I called the meeting tonight to talk to Siren about the takeover of Green River. Before she gets here, tell me your thoughts," Malachi wanted to know as he stared each of us in the eyes.

"I don't give a fuck what Siren says, I'm taking all those Green River niggas out. They the niggas that been robbing the traps. And, I know y'all noticed our niggas disappearing around this bitch. I don't even know why we gotta have a meeting about this when we could be riding on them pussy niggas right now." I was the first to speak. All this shit had me all stressed out, and a meeting was the last thing I wanted to be attending with all that had been going on.

No one said anything; instead, they just looked from me to Malachi, who sat rubbing his temples. He spoke slowly like he was trying to keep control of himself.

"Bro, if our team is missing, what team we taking with us to ride on Green River?" he asked, glaring at me.

Before I could answer, there were three knocks at the door; Siren's signal. I scooted my chair back to go and open it like I usually did, but Malachi stood too.

"Dame, keep this shit professional. Whatever y'all do outside of this is on y'all. I just hope she ain't on no petty bullshit," he said to me.

"Troy, go let her in. Dame, sit down." I glared at this nigga.

He must've thought he brought Danger, his pit bull, 'cause I knew damn good and well he wasn't talking to me like no damn dog. I was about to argue, but Troy had already opened the door.

"What's up, girl— GOT DAMN!" Troy yelled.

I heard her giggle. "Hey, Troy," she said, giving him a light hug. He stepped to the side and allowed her to enter. My eyes ballooned when I peeped what she was wearing.

She had on some spiky heels that allowed two of her freshly polished toes to peep through on each foot. Her oiled legs looked long as shit, going up miles to the tiniest black shorts that looked like they could pass for fucking panties. I could see her pussy print easily. Her stomach was flat and bare, and she wore some type of gold and diamond jewelry that wrapped around her waist. Over her chest was a black studded bra that had her breasts pushed to her damn chin. The tattoos that ran down the left side of her body were on full display. There was a black sheer piece connected to the back of her bra top that hung down her back like a cape. Upon closer inspection, it was almost like black wings protruding from her shoulder blades. Her face was beautiful as usual, but she had on some dark eye makeup that made her reddish-brown eyes look like fire. She wore that red lip gloss that I knew for a fact tasted like cherries, because I had tasted it before.

Her dreads were neatly twisted and styled. Siren carried a tan bookbag that I knew, from previous meetings, had all her magic supplies. The room was quiet as all my brothers pretty much eye-fucked her. My blood was boiling, but my dick was rock hard. I wanted to kill this bitch, bring her back to life, and fuck the dog shit out of her. When she walked, her breasts jiggled and hypnotized a nigga as she walked right past me and headed to Malachi to give him a hug. I took the opportunity to glance at her ass, as did the rest of my brothers. She had her flawless backside on full display. I glanced at Marsean and raised my brow. He shook his head and whispered.

"Nigga, you stupid for fucking this one up." Slowly, she walked around the table, hugging everyone except me.

Once she was done showing off, she took her seat. No one said anything for a minute, and the tension was thick as fuck in the room. Finally, Malachi cleared his throat.

"Damn, Siren. A nigga didn't mean to call you away from a Victoria's Secret show."

She giggled. "I have an engagement after this," she informed the room.

He raised his brow. "You not doing business with nobody else, right?" he asked her.

She shook her head. "Nah, it's not business. It's personal." He paused and looked from her to me.

I was gritting her ass, but she wouldn't even look in my direction. She was sitting there examining her nails like shit was sweet.

"Bitch, if—" I started, but Malachi cut me off.

"DAME, SIT DOWN!" he roared.

"Nah! Fuck that!" I yelled, running around the table and snatching her up.

"Get off me, Dame," she stated calmly.

"You on your petty shit, huh? You think you gonna go spread your legs for the next nigga?"

This bitch had the nerve to laugh. I choke-slammed her into the wall and heard chairs scooting and footsteps running toward us. My brothers were all trying to get me off her, but nobody could move me. I had a stronghold on her neck. Her hair started floating and wiggling around her and before my eyes, her dreads turned into long, shiny black snakes with red heads. They reared back and struck, biting me on my face, neck, arms and hands. That shit felt like fire flowing through my blood every time they bit me. I unwrapped my hands from her throat to swat them away, and they quickly coiled around my neck. I reached for her again but before I could grip her, her snakes slammed me on the floor, still choking me. I was partially blacking out, losing air at a rapid pace, but still fighting for consciousness. I heard a gun cock.

"Siren, I look at you like a sister, but if you don't call your pets off my fucking brother, I'll blow your head off!" Marsean's voice rang out. Slowly, her hair unwound from my neck and quickly shot over to Marsean, snatched his gun, and flung it across the room. I was still on the floor struggling for breath as she stepped over my body, heels clicking on the floor, and walked back to her seat.

"Well, you niggas fucked my hair up and now I'm pissed. Can we please get down to business because as I said earlier, I have some place to be!" she yelled with her back to us.

This bitch was crazy, crazier than I thought. Troy reached down to help me up, but I smacked his hand away and sat up. I examined my hands and saw all the tiny bite marks that were already starting to swell, and I knew my face probably looked just as bad.

I flexed my fingers, making sure they still had movement as my brothers waited to see what I would do. I stood, angrily snatched out a chair, and sat directly across from her. She folded her arms and glared at me while I glared at her. When I noticed the light bruising starting to form around her neck, I felt like shit.

"Baby..." I started.

She had tears in her eyes as she held her hand up to silence me. "Dame," Malachi warned.

Once everyone was seated, Malachi began again. "Si, we want Green River." She nodded and began unpacking her supplies. We watched as she lit the candles, poured the water, and flicked open her knife. She glanced at me as she did that. I smirked, not scared at all her thinly veiled threats. If anything, the shit was starting to turn me on.

She clapped her hands and the lights shut off, leaving only the flickering candles for sight. She made a deep cut in her hand and allowed it to drip into her cup.

"Spirits, we need guidance. Please come to us," she spoke loudly.

Within seconds, it felt as if the room was filled with people. Whispers and murmurs could be heard from every direction. "Is there anything standing in the way of these men gaining territory from Green River?" she asked.

I watched her listen to the whispers. She looked at all of us. "Which of you has acquired an enemy from Green River?" she asked.

We all looked at each other. I sighed, "A nigga from Green River been hitting my traps," I answered.

"I should've known it was you," she mumbled under her breath. "Is there any other way?" She asked the invisible motherfuckers around us.

Sitting down, she grabbed one of the hand mirrors and blew on it. She watched intently for a few moments before slamming the mirror face down.

"Thank you," she said. and the room cleared. The lights flickered on shortly after. Siren took her time blowing out each candle while we waited for her to say something. She stared at me and a tear fell from her eye. This shit wasn't going to be good.

Taking a deep breath, she spoke. "If you go against Green River right now... you'll die. There army is strong, consisting mostly of shifters. Your team is too small. Rebuild Bellmont first, then in one year, go for the takeover."

I shook my head. "Fuck that. We moving now!" I yelled.

She began packing away her supplies. "The spirits have spoken."

"I don't give a fuck!" I yelled at her.

"Dame, shut the fuck up!" Malachi sternly yelled at me.

She shook her head and slammed the mirror on the table. "This is your fate. If you move now, asshole!"

We all leaned over the table to look at the mirror. I watched Marsean take numerous bullets to his back and collapse. Malachi had his heart ripped out by a shifter, while I was chained to a wall taking blow after blow to my face. My jaw hung limply, and I could tell it was dislocated. Someone finally put me out of my misery with a bullet to the head.

"What the fuck?" Marsean yelled.

I grabbed the mirror and threw it against the wall, causing it to shatter all over the floor, the sound echoing throughout the empty warehouse.

"Do what I said, and wait a year. Rebuild," Siren repeated herself, speaking to Malachi.

He nodded and handed her a thick envelope that I knew was filled with cash. Slipping it into her knapsack, she stood.

"Gentlemen... and Dame," she threw shade. "I can't do this for you anymore. I'm leaving Bellmont for good. I wish you the best, and I'll leave you with my protection oil... but, I just can't do this anymore," she informed us as she glanced at me when she said the last part.

"Siren, if this has anything to do with Dame and the baby, you can just meet with me and I'll relay the message. I'll double your pay," Malachi bargained with her.

I was hot this nigga brought the baby up because I saw Siren cringe when he said it.

"I appreciate that, Malachi, but I just can't." With that, she grabbed her things and hurried out the building.

"Troy, can you make sure she gets to her car alright?" I asked my brother.

He shrugged, "I'm sure Medusa don't need no help, but I'll check." He stood up and went to go make sure Siren got to her bed.

I could feel Malachi gritting me. "What?" I yelled at him.

"Yo, I knew you was gonna fuck this up. That's your fault, nigga, that she ain't working with us no more."

I flipped the table over because I had no more words left to give, and because I knew he was right. I left to head outside because I needed to cool down before I did something stupid. I leaned against Marsean's truck and sparked some weed. He came out a few minutes later and just stood in front of me.

"You good?" he asked.

I nodded as the smoke filled my lungs. "I will be." I was going to get Siren back on my team, no matter what it took.

11

MEGA

*I*t had been almost a week since I seen Siren. I knew I had to go to her soon for training. I promised her father that I would watch out for her, but never would I have thought that the gods would make her my mate. Now, I was struggling with the desire I felt for her and the promise I made her father years ago. Twenty-four years ago, the shifters of Green River took it upon themselves to kill Leo without my stamp of approval. It was a crime for a shifter to breed with a human, but because Leo fell for a human witch, there were some loopholes that I was working on. Leo was a smart and loyal friend to me. He never hesitated whenever we went to battle. You would be surprised how many people would eventually show their true colors when you lived to be over two thousand years old. I've seen plenty shifters turn from friend to foe over time. The night they killed him, I felt in my gut something was wrong. I ran for miles, trying to get to him but by the time I got there, he was so far gone that even my blood couldn't bring him back.

He asked about his family, and I told him they had got away. He asked me to look out for Siren and Mike, but especially Siren since she was just a baby. I told him I would and right after that, he died in my arms. It took me awhile to even find where Willow had taken the kids, as she was using citrus to cover up their scents. After I murdered the shifters involved with the death of Leo, I made it my mission to find Siren. It wasn't until I got a call about a mangled body found in the woods that I caught my first whiff of her. When I arrived, I wrongly assumed it had to be Bear, one of my alphas. Bear wasn't smart or brave or any of the qualities that a normal alpha possessed, but his father was the previous alpha. His father was also one of the shifters I killed behind Leo's death. I decided not to interfere and let him have it, but I kept close tabs on him. I had just ended a meeting with him, and that little ungrateful motherfucker caused me to shift twice. I knew sooner or later, I would have to kill him for his lack of respect. I let him off with a warning tonight; a broken jaw.

I walked out of my hotel suite in Green River and prepared for the ten-mile run to get to Siren. It was about one-thirty in the morning; the moon was full and the night was quiet, except for the little nocturnal creatures that came alive when the sun went down. It was close to two in the morning when her building came into view. I could smell her the closer I got. She thought she was covering her scent with that citrus shit she lathered herself in, but because I was chosen to be her mate, I could smell her pussy whenever she was turned on, which seemed to be quite often. It was a mixture of honey, Amber, and musk. It drove me fucking crazy. I climbed up the wall using my sharp claws for support and stopped at her fourth-floor window. Her curtains were closed, but the window was cracked open and her scent wafted out to me, beckoning me.

I took a deep breath in and reminded myself to practice self-control, and block my mind from her nosey ass. I tried to knock on her window, but I couldn't fit my paw through the security bars. Annoyed, I snatched them off and tossed them over my shoulder. The metal hit the ground with a clang noise, causing a few stray cats to scatter. Even though it was pitch black in there, I could still make out her silhouette. She was sitting up in her bed and looking in my direction. I could hear her lightly sniffing the air.

"Mega?" she asked in this sleepy, yet husky voice.

My dick shot up and banged against the wall, knocking a few

pieces of stone out of place. *Down boy*, I thought to myself. I couldn't speak when I was in shifter form, so I communicated through thought.

"It's me, Siren. Come to the window."

She clicked on a light and padded over to where I was. She pulled apart the curtains and gasped as she backed away. I was huge in shifter form and it could be shocking, even to other shifters.

"It's me, baby. You making me feel ugly out here." I thought, joking with her.

Quickly, she opened the window and screen, allowing me to fit my snout and part of my head into her window. My nose accidentally bumped into her thigh, and her smell shot straight up my nostrils, causing me to drool a bit.

"You're beautiful," she said in awe while softly rubbing my fur.

I took a good look at her wearing a tiny white undershirt and some blue panties. I felt my dick jump again and bang into the wall below me.

"What was that?" she asked. "Are you ok? Want me to pull you in?"

I shook my head. There was no way I would fit through this window without caving in half of her wall.

"I won't fit. I want you to come outside with me so we can start your training."

She frowned her cute face up. "What training? Nigga, it's two in the morning."

I laughed at her. *"This is the best time to train."*

"Well, let me freshen up and throw on some clothes first," she finally obliged.

"Freshen up, but you won't need any clothes."

She raised her brow and looked at me. "I mean, you're going to be shifting, clothes are pointless," I added.

She just smiled and walked into her bathroom. This was going to be hard, I could already tell. We wanted each other too bad. I eased out of her window and jumped down to the ground, landing on all fours. I paced a bit, while waiting for her, until I smelled her back at the window. I looked up at her.

"Jump down," I told her, positioning myself right under her window.

"What? I have a door, Mega!" she yelled.

"You have to learn to trust me. Jump. I won't let you hit the ground." She shut off her lights and swung her legs out of the window.

I heard her take a deep breath, then she jumped, landing right on my back. Damn, it felt good to feel her this close!

"Hold on tight." She pressed her body flat against me and gripped my fur.

When I felt that she had a good grip, I took off full speed while Siren screamed and laughed.

"This reminds me of that movie, *Never-ending story*! she screamed out. "Go Falkor!" she screamed while pumping a fist in the air.

I laughed while jumping over cars and dumpsters like it was nothing. Once we hit the woods, I jumped from sturdy tree top to tree top, until I found a clearing. I had an adrenaline rush, so I let out a long howl before I jumped down to the clearing and sat low, so she could climb off my back. I stood up straight and shifted into my human form. I stared at Siren, who was still in her panties and under-shirt, while I stood in front of her naked. Even in human form, I was blessed, and it was evident from Siren's stares that she had never seen anything like this.

"Oh my God," she whispered.

Siren, I... Siren! Up here." I pointed to my eyes. Once I had her attention, I started again. "I want to see you shift," I told her.

I walked closer to her and caressed her soft skin. "Your body reacts to me because I'm your mate," I revealed to her.

Her eyes widened. "So, it is true!" she exclaimed.

I nodded my head and stepped closer to her. "Your body does what I tell it to... now, shift."

Just like that, her bones began snapping and cracking. I wasn't sure how big she would get, so I backed up to give her space. I watched as she sprouted long, red razor-like claws and sharp white teeth. Shiny blue-black fur grew instantly all over her body. By the time she finished, I was in amazement at how perfect she was. She was big, not as big as I was in wolf form, but she was definitely a larger one. Her eyes glowed bright yellow, and she was midnight blue everywhere except for the tips of her ears and a circle around the end of her tail, which was bright red. She licked her paw and smoothed her hair around her face, which caused me to laugh. I walked over to her and touched her face. Her hair felt like silk. I struggled to keep myself from shifting because I wanted to mate with her right now. I never seen a shifter as beautiful as she was right in this moment.

"Well, what do you think?" she spoke to me in her thoughts since she couldn't speak.

"You're perfect," I told her with no hesitation, "The gods took their time when they formed you," I added, rubbing the red tip of her ear.

"You're not so bad yourself."

I smiled. "You know that feeling you get when you shift? That ball of energy that surrounds you?" I asked.

"Yes."

"I want you to remember that feeling but instead of letting it go, hold it tight and place it back inside of yourself."

She cocked her head to the side. *"Okay."*

After about a minute or two, I watched her change back to human form.

"Wow!" she yelled.

I couldn't say anything because I was too busy taking in her body. She was bad as a motherfucker. My dick noticed as well 'cause he was standing up, trying to get a better view. Her smell was driving me crazy and when I couldn't take it anymore, I grabbed her arm and pulled her to me roughly. She stumbled over some sticks, but I caught her and tongue-kissed her deeply. Siren moaned in my mouth and ran her nails lightly over my chest while I pressed her tighter into my body. I wanted her to feel how hard I was. Cupping her ass, I made her spread her legs. Never breaking our hungry kiss, I lifted her up as she wrapped her long, smooth legs around me. I dropped to the ground, still holding her, and positioned myself over top of her. Foreplay crossed my mind, but I felt like if I didn't slide inside of her this minute, I was going to combust.

I positioned myself at her wet entrance and nuzzled her neck, remembering that was a sensitive spot from our first encounter, and I slid in inch by inch. She screamed and clawed my back as I stretched her. I had to keep telling myself to take it easy because she was untouched, but once I was halfway in, she tried to scoot back.

"Unnhhh. Oh my God, Mega, it's too much. I can't take it!" she squealed.

"Yes, you can!" I growled, gripping her thighs and slamming all twelve inches inside of her.

"AHHHHH!" She screamed and pounded on my chest as I went completely still, letting her get used to my size.

I kissed her neck and made my way down to her breasts, until I heard her moan and she started writhing under me. Easing in and out of her slowly, I allowed her to match my rhythm. I spread her legs further and went deeper.

"Does it feel better now?" I whispered in her ear.

"Ummm hmmm, oh God, yesssss," she moaned.

Hearing her moan made me go harder. She felt better than I imagined. I could feel her body pulsating.

"I'm coming, Mega! Please don't stop!" she yelled.

I had no intention of stopping. With one hand, she gripped my shoulder, digging her nails in while her other hand gripped the earth beside her. I reached down and played with her clit until she squirted over both of us. She was done, but I wasn't. I tossed one of her legs over my shoulder and dug as deep as I could. Her pussy muscles tightening around me had my nut building up. I wanted to make sure I was as deep as I could go when I released in her. Afterward, my dick swelled up inside of her and I couldn't pull it out without hurting her, so we laid there like that for a few minutes, catching our breath, kissing on each other, and inhaling each other's scent. After about ten minutes, the swelling went down and we decided to go swimming in the river to clean off. Then, we shifted and chased each other back to her building. I climbed up to her floor with her following, and I shifted so I could fit in her window. She then shifted so I could pull her in. We took a hot shower together and as she soaped my back, she asked me how old I was.

"How old do I look?" I countered her question with another question. I turned around and wiped the water down my face.

"You look about twenty-nine or thirty, but as a shifter, you could be thousands of years old," she guessed, staring at me intently.

I nodded my head. "I'm twenty-three thousand years old."

"Dammnnn, you old as dirt!"

I laughed, flicking some water on her. "I'm the oldest of our kind."

She bombarded me with question after question.

I scooped her up and carried her out of the bathroom. "Can you feed me first? I burnt off a lot of energy in the woods. Feed me and I'll tell you everything I know."

Throwing her head back, she laughed loudly and grabbed my hand. She led me to her kitchen, where I took a seat and watched intently as her ass moved and bounced around through her silk robe as she made our plates. She didn't know she was in for a long night.

Setting the food and a bottle of water in front of me, she said, "Now, talk nigga. I wanna know everything."

I chuckled, shook my head, and started at the beginning, telling her everything.

12

SIREN

I didn't wake up until twelve in the afternoon. As soon as I opened my eyes, I felt pain shoot through every part of my body. Between all the shifting, fucking, and running, my body was exhausted. Mega told me his whole story, and I didn't know if I should thank the gods or my father for sending me this perfect man. We talked all night and I could have listened to him talk forever, except we kept stopping to fuck. This motherfucker called himself taking it easy and making love after I complained from the soreness, and it started off easy with soft kisses and touching. You know, just getting acquainted with each other's bodies, but within fifteen minutes, his big ass was digging in me like my pussy was gold. He ended up cracking my oak headboard. I rolled over and stared at him, just taking in his bone structure, pretty chocolate skin, and long lashes. He was so perfect.

"That shit is weird," he mumbled and rolled over.

I laughed and climbed on top of him. He chuckled, pushed me onto the bed and climbed over me, attacking my face and neck with his soft lips. My phone vibrated on the nightstand, interrupting our play-fighting session. Reaching for it, I looked at the message from

Gee telling me she would be here in five minutes. We were supposed to be going house hunting.

"Dammit, Mega. You got me sleeping all late, forgot I'm going house shopping with my girlfriend." He frowned his face

"House shopping? We're mated. You have to stay with me," he nonchalantly replied.

"What? I need to stay close to my mother," I said. "Her magic's not as strong as it used to be," I explained to him.

"We'll get a house close to your mom," he shrugged.

"What about Gee?" I asked.

"I got it. Don't worry. And you don't have to wear that citrus shit anymore. I left my essence all on you... and in you," he said, kissing my neck and making me giggle.

"We have to get dressed," I said. He stood and stretched.

"I came here naked," he said. I looked at his immaculate form and wondered if, maybe, I had time for a quickie.

"You don't," He smirked.

"Get out of my head!" I yelled. Because we mated, we could read each other's thoughts at will and get this... I couldn't block him. "Anyway," I said, cutting my eyes at him. "I don't have any men's clothes here—"

"You better not," he said seriously.

I rolled my eyes. "As I was saying. Let me try something." I pointed my finger at him and formed a white, silky button-down shirt, and some matching white pants with some hot sneakers. I left a few of his buttons undone and placed a gold chain with a wolf medallion on it around his neck. "Perfect!" I yelled, pumping my fist in the air.

He looked down at his clothes with large eyes. "I look like a R&B album." I fell on the floor, laughing my ass off at the fifth Jodeci member. He shook his head. "How long will this last?" he asked.

"Just until you get home. It's only a glamour," I told him.

He walked over to me and tossed me in the air before catching me in his arms. He nuzzled his nose into my neck, inhaling.

"I'm going to text you an address, go there today. And, I'll see you tonight," he said, placing me back down on my feet and kissing me so deeply I started to get dizzy.

"OK," I said. "Were you serious about me not covering my scent?" I asked.

"Yeah. None of the shifters will fuck with you once they smell my scent on you. Don't worry about anything," he told me, kissing me again.

I walked him to the door and as soon as he opened it, Gee was standing there about to knock. Her mouth hung open in shock as she stared at him. I told y'all he was fine.

"You must be Gee?" he chuckled, looking at her and then at me as I tried to hold my laugh in.

"I think she's starstruck, you fake Idris!" I thought.

He laughed loudly and told Gee it was nice to meet her before kissing me again and reminding me to check my text messages for the address as he headed down the stairs. Finally, Gee cleared her throat.

"I'm Gee," she said weakly down the steps.

"Bitch! He gone. Get your ass in here." I laughed. "Hoe, I oughta kick your ass for drooling after my man."

"Your man?" she exclaimed, stepping inside and closing the door. "Wait! Was that the... is he the... shifter? Dammnn! Bitch, I would've risked it all too!" she yelled, high-fiving me. "I can smell it in here."

I was shocked! I didn't know humans could smell shifters!

"You can smell his scent?" I asked.

"No girl! I smell pussy, ass, and sweat! Open your damn windows!"

I laughed and as she went around opening windows, I got ready to take a shower.

"You got laid! I want details!" she yelled.

"I will! Let me wash my ass first!" I said, grabbing a new towel and heading to the bathroom.

"Ummm Si, what happened to your window?"

I ignored her and closed the bathroom door. Just as I was about to turn the water on, I heard her voice at the door "Ummm Si, what happened to your headboard?!"

Laughing to myself, I hopped in the shower. Once I was dressed in a mini white eyelet dress and some nude heels, I walked into the living room. Gee immediately turned off the *Love and Hip Hop* reruns she was watching and turned her full attention to me.

"Aight, bitch— give me the tea, and don't leave anything out!" she squealed, grabbing a pillow. I started from when his smell woke me out of my sleep and told her the whole story. Her eyes were huge by the end. "Was he really that big, or are you exaggerating?" she asked me.

I held up my hand and shook my head.

"Girl he's huge! I thought I was gonna die at first! Could you imagine somebody finding my body in the woods just ripped right down the middle? But, after a while..." I paused, reminiscing, "Girl, it just felt amazing. Like, the best feeling I've ever felt."

"It's only going to get better," Mega's deep voice boomed in my head.

"Oh my God! Get out of my head! Weren't you the one who told me it's not polite to read people's thoughts?"

"I was only checking to see if you went to the address I sent."

"Nigga, you've been gone an hour. You know damn well we ain't left yet. Take your thirsty ass on!" I yelled at him in my head.

He laughed loudly. *"I see Imma have to teach your disrespectful mouth a lesson when I see you tonight.201D*

I instantly had a vision of me trying to fit all his dick down my throat and became aroused.

"Wow! I'm just hype that we both dating shifters! Ayyyeee!" Gee said.

"Twinning!" I yelled as we both did our happy dance, which consisted of twerks and spins. "Wait! Gee, what shifter you dating?" I asked, suddenly realizing I didn't know what in the hell she was talking about.

She sat back down and gave me a sly smile. "Well, Mike and I have been kicking it since we left here together the day that bitch sliced my tires." My eyes were about to pop out of my head.

I knew Gee has had a crush on my brother since I could remember, so I was happy for her, but I also knew Mike was a big-time hoe. I made a mental note to call him and make sure he wasn't going to fuck my friend over. In the meantime, I was gonna be a good friend.

"Awwww Gee, I'm so happy for you. Give me... details," I said, trying to stop myself from gagging.

She looked at me for a moment, "Girl, I know your ass don't want details," she said, laughing.

I let out a deep breath and laughed too. "Let's go. Ain't you gonna put on your peach grapefruit lotion?" she asked, gathering her purse.

I shook my head. "Mega said it's not needed anymore."

"Are you sure?" she asked. I nodded my head

"Yup, and I actually want to try it out. Let's go."

OUTSIDE WAS STILL A GHOST TOWN. Two guys were out, Drew being one of them.

"We taking your car or mine?" Gee inquired.

"Let's take yours," I said, glancing at Drew.

"Just give me one minute," I told her as she nodded and walked toward her cherry red Maxima.

I threw my purse over my shoulder and headed over to Drew. His eyes widened as he looked around nervously before they landed on me. He jumped up so quickly, he knocked over the carton he was sitting on. "Hey, Drew!" I said cheerily.

"H-hey, Siren," he said, keeping his head down.

"Have you noticed no one's been out lately?" I asked, gesturing toward the empty corners. He still wouldn't pick his head up, but I could see his nose twitching. I knew he could smell Mega on me.

"I heard a couple niggas got knocked," he lied. Gianna was the hood anchorwoman, and she would've known if there had been mass arrests and already dished to me.

"Ummm hmmm. Ok Drew, I'll see you around," I said, ending the conversation, because suddenly, I didn't feel comfortable.

Knowing that the Green River shifters killed my father, had beef with Dame, and niggas from my way were going missing while a Green River shifter sat here chilling wasn't sitting to well with me. Sliding into the passenger side of Gee's car, I glanced back to see Drew busy on his phone. I was glad I was moving soon because this didn't feel right. Grabbing my phone, I rattled off the address to Gee to plug into her GPS.

"Wayment, this is North Bellmont. That's like twenty-minutes from your mom! Girl, I can't afford those mini mansions! You know I'm in nursing school and only working part-time right now. I thought we were going to look at those family homes they just built on the outskirts of the jects?" she said.

"I did too, but Mega wants us to check out this place."

"Guess it can't hurt to look," she said, shrugging her shoulders.

"Gee, have you heard anything 'bout dudes getting knocked back to back?"

She shook her head, "Knocked? No. Missing persons. Yes! I thought Dame and them would've told you! Damn near half of their team is fuckin' MIA!" she replied, glancing between me and the road.

"I knew something happened, but I didn't know exactly what it was."

"Honestly, I think it's a shifter," she whispered. I took notice of the fact that this bitch could whisper when it was just me and her in a car, but she just couldn't keep her voice down in a crowded restaurant.

"I do too," I said.

About forty-five minutes later, we pulled up to the address and both of our jaws hit the ground. The mansion sat up on a hill surrounded by trees, and we slowly drove up the driveway that split into two lanes and circled around the property. We looked at each other before hopping out to examine the outside. I noticed a silver BMW parked on the other side and wondered if someone was living here.

Walking through the path that separated the lush garden, I

noticed statues of different animals and lots of small fountains that led to a giant pool. I spotted what looked like a national park behind the pool. I looked up and noticed another house almost as big as the main one, and they were connected by a huge screened in deck.

"Oh my God, girl you see this?" I asked. When she didn't respond, I turned around to see her posing for a selfie in front of the pool. I laughed at her duck lips. "Gianna! What if somebody lives here?"

Just then, the door opened and an older honey-colored man walked down the steps. He was wearing a three-piece gray suit and was smiling.

"No one lives here as of yet. I'm Marcus, a real estate agent for Mr. Bradley. If you're done looking around outside, Ms. Falls, I'd love to show you two around inside," he said.

I held out my hand for him to shake, "Please, call me Siren, and this is Gianna," I pointed to Gee, who had walked up now.

She smiled and held her hand out. "As I'm sure you've noticed, these are two homes on a shared property," he spoke, leading us up onto the porch.

We surveyed the smaller home first, which was absolutely immaculate, and then headed back across to the larger one that was filled with spiraling staircases, huge ceiling to floor windows, and balconies. Back in the kitchen, I looked out the picture window and stared at the bright garden and deep woods. I wanted this house. *Fuck those family homes, I want this one*, I decided.

"Marcus, how much is this property going for?" I asked.

"$2.7 million, which is actually a good deal, considering." We both looked at Gee, who jumped up and grabbed her purse. I held up a finger, signaling for her to wait.

"What's the down payment?" I asked.

"$450,000."

Damn. This was going to wipe me almost completely out. It would leave me with exactly a little change to start a business with. Maybe I would call Malachi and continue to work with just him. He did say he would double my pay. I could invest the money I had left and still have income from him. Reaching into my purse, I pulled out my checkbook.

"Siren! Can you do this?" Gee asked.

I nodded my head and began to fill out the check. I was still going over the numbers in my head as I got to the signature line.

"Ms. Falls... Siren. You don't have to do that." I looked up at him, confused.

Did he want to sell the house or not? He smiled at the confusion on my face and shook his head. "This house already belongs to you. Mr. Bradley purchased it earlier today," he informed me and nodded his head over my shoulder. I turned and saw Mega swaggering toward me like he owned the place... well technically, I guess he did.

"You like it?" he asked about the home, but I didn't miss the sexual undertones.

"I love it," I said.

"Gee, you cool with your side?" he asked, motioning with his thumb toward the porch and the other house.

"WHAT?!" she yelled excitedly, causing Marcus to jump a little. I chuckled.

Mega nodded his head, "I couldn't split y'all up, but my girl can't be in the jects too much longer. It's not safe anymore."

I glanced up at him when he said that. I wondered if he knew something. I tried to ease in his mind, and I saw flashes of my conversation with Drew. Mega glanced at me.

"We move in next week; they still have a few finishing touches to do," he said to me, then focused his attention on Marcus and Gee.

"Marcus, why don't you give Gee another tour of her home."

He smiled. "Of course," he said and held his hand out to help Gee up. She had this stupid smile on her face ever since she found out the adjoining house was hers.

Once they left, I turned to Mega, preparing to fire off question after question, but before I could get a word out, he kissed me, backing me all the way up onto the stainless-steel island in the center of the kitchen. His hands ran all over my body and stopped on my ass. He was kissing me so intensely, it was becoming hard to breathe, but I wasn't complaining. Shit, take my breath away. Pulling my dress up around my waist, he lifted me and slammed me down on the counter, and the cold metal against my warm thighs sent quick shockwaves through my body. Standing in between my legs, he used my hips to pull me to the edge, until my pantiless center was rubbing against his jean-clad dick. Once he broke our kiss, I used the opportunity to take in a large breath as he dropped down in front of me. Hungrily, he dove face first into my pussy and began eating me like he was starving. It hadn't even been a minute, and I was on the verge of cumming.

"Uhnnnnn," I yelled, failing miserably at trying to keep quiet.

I came and tried to squirm away, but he held his grip on my hips and kept going. His tongue was winding around inside of me while his teeth kept grazing my clit, causing me to explode again in a matter of minutes. After he licked all my juices up, he loosened his grip and stood over me.

"I caught that little image you had earlier," he growled in my ear. "Do it now," he said, pulling me to my feet.

I knew exactly what he was referring to, so I dropped to my knees, hurriedly unzipped his jeans, and pulled out his perfect dick. Licking my lips, I admired every pulsating vein with my fingertips before spitting on it and slowly sucking the head into my wet mouth. Steadily, I pulled him down my throat inch by inch, until I was comfortable with his size, then I sped up the pace. I made sure his head rubbed against the roof of my mouth every time I sucked him down. I relaxed my throat, but tightened my jaws and slurped all over it.

"SHIT!" he yelled, gripping the bun that was neatly pulled up on my head, then he began fucking my face. I made sure to lock my throat muscles right after he plunged in so it would be harder for him to pull out.

On the last stroke, he yelled out and released down my throat, and I turned into a vacuum and sucked every drop out of him. He tasted as good as he smelled. I swallowed everything in my mouth and ran my tongue along the underside of his dick as I leisurely allowed him to slide out of my mouth.

"Gotdamn!" he said, trying to catch his breath while I silently patted myself on the back.

He lifted me to my feet and quickly bent me over the island. I made sure to arch my back as he plunged into me deeply, causing me to cry out from the initial shock of his size. He was way too deep, so I tried to scoot up to alleviate some of the pressure, but he grabbed my waist and pulled me to him hard.

"Mega!" I begged.

"Don't run now! I gotta teach you to respect your alpha! What was the shit you was talking earlier?" he demanded, wrapping my hair around his hand. I shook my head.

"AHHH! Nothing! I promise! I'll do better, daddy! Mega, PLEASE!"

"Too late!" he yelled, snatching my hair and causing my head to jerk up as my ass raised higher while he pounded into me, mercilessly, putting constant pressure on my G-spot, causing me to explode back to back until I was drained.

He let my hair go and I tried to crawl away, but he grabbed both of my legs and lifted them off the floor so that my upper body was lying flat on the island as he had control of my lower body. He entered me from a different angle and stroked slow, but each time he entered, he went deeper until he was buried inside of me. This new angle was sending chills all through my body, and I could feel my juices running down my legs. He was holding me on the brink of an orgasm. I squeezed my eyes shut and felt the tears slip out.

"Mega, please," I whined hoarsely.

"Please, what?" he taunted, still diving deep.

"Please make me cum, Mega!"

He went faster, and the friction was better than heaven as I felt myself falling. "Fuuccckkk!" I moaned, as my body started convulsing like I was having seizures.

With each shake, my pussy muscles clenched down and I could feel exactly how deep he was planted inside my tunnel, which caused me to ride this orgasm long as fuck! Shit seemed never-ending! At the same time, I felt him swell and erupt inside me as he let out a long, deep growl and dug his fingers, almost painfully, into my legs.

He collapsed on top of my back and gently moved my hair to the side. "You gonna stop talking crazy to me?" he asked.

"Ummm hmmm," I whined and nodded my head.

It was now my mission in life to talk crazy to him as much as I possibly could.

13

BEAR

Drew: Nigga I'm out. Baby Black's chick came outside smelling just like Mega. He marked her. From what I hear, the Black cartel ain't even worried about Green River no more, so what am I still doing here?

Me: Motherfucker, I don't give a fuck about the Black cartel. We going after somebody heavier. I want Mega's head. So, you'll stay right the fuck there 'til I tell you what to do, nigga.

Drew: Mega!? Nah nigga, I want no parts.

Me: Really, nigga? This how you talk to your alpha? How 'bout I kill yo' bitch?

Drew: Bear, just hit me with the plan.

That's what the fuck I thought. Ol' bitch ass nigga. If a nigga threatened my bitch, I wouldn't be worried at all 'cause my bitch was trained to go. I made her that way. I beat her ass so much that she could go toe to toe with me. There was always a method to my madness. I slammed my phone down on the sink and looked at my face in the mirror. My jaw was broken a few days ago, thanks to that nut nigga Mega, but it was healing fast. Now, it was just swollen. I was still fine as hell. I used this pretty boy swag shit to my advantage. Underneath this light skin and curly hair, I was a motherfuckin' monster and nobody ever saw me coming. I was going to take Mega down and take his place, and he just made the shit that much easier for me by falling into some pussy. He was one of them old school niggas that mated for life, so I knew he would be on his captain save a hoe and try to move hell and high water if I snatched his bitch. The fact that she was with that nigga Dame, I could use that nigga to help. Since she's a witch, I knew she probably had a bunch of tricks up her sleeve, but I had something for her ass. I'm sure he would be happy to help once he heard his bitch was fucking a big ass shifter. She probably getting her pussy all stretched the fuck out. I scanned through my phone, looking at the pictures Drew sent me of the witch. She was bad as fuck. I stared at the one of her walking away, and her ass was fat as shit. Maybe after I killed Mega and that nigga Dame, just because, I would spare her life and put her on the team. Then again, I didn't know; she had a bad reputation for fucking with these lames. I might kill her too, depending on my mood. I was definitely going to hit up Dame tomorrow and make him an offer he couldn't refuse.

It was a little after two in the morning when wifey came strolling in from the club smelling like liquor, weed, and the random niggas that she let dance on her. I walked out of the bedroom and down the stairs to meet her at the door. Lele used to be a bad bitch. I mean, she still was but she loved to snort coke, blow weed and drink, and it was starting to take its toll on her. She wasn't like this when we first met and mated. I could admit that I played a small part in it since I introduced her to the powder. She wasn't freaky enough when we fucked, so I thought the coke would help loosen her up. Right now, she was fine as fuck, standing about 5'7 with rich honey brown skin. Her skin glowed, but I knew it was an illusion of makeup. When she washed her face, her dark eye circles and dull skin would return. She had honey blonde, shoulder length dreads and bright green eyes that gave her the appearance of a lion. She used to be thick, but over the years, she lost a lot of weight. She was slim with slight curves.

"Bitch, why the fuck is you always out?" I spat.

She looked at me and sniffed. "Don't start with me, Bear." I shook my head in disgust.

"Always out partying and shit, probably the reason you can't have no fucking babies!" I shouted.

She narrowed her eyes. "Did you ever think maybe it's yo' dick that's the problem! I know you fucking other bitches and none of them popped up pregnant!" she screamed.

I popped her in her mouth. "Bitch, keep your voice down! We got neighbors!"

She moved her hand from her mouth and surveyed the blood on her fingers. "I'm so happy I never had kids by you! You're a disgrace to the pack!" she spat.

I raised my fist to hit her again, but she clocked me in my nose before I could strike. I stumbled back, feeling the sting from her hit. She went to run up the stairs, but I grabbed her by the back of her neck and threw her to the floor, then started stomping her in the chest. I left her balled up on the floor crying and went upstairs to the bedroom and locked the door. Her ass could sleep on the couch tonight.

I WOKE up the next day, and Lele called herself giving me the silent treatment. It was taking everything in me not to kill her. At one time, I did love her but the longer I stayed, the more I realized she wasn't suited to be an alpha mate. I could do better.

"What's for breakfast?" I asked her. Silence.

I glanced at her standing at the sink. She had on a V-neck tee shirt, and I could see the purple and black bruises on her chest from where she made me stomp her. See, that's the bullshit. Like, why would you put on a V-neck? You trying to showcase your bruises? I hated when she played that victim shit. I sat at the table, pulled out my phone, and texted her sister, Maya.

"Who you texting, Bear?" she asked. I raised my brow.

"Oh, you can speak now? Where the fuck is my food, Le?" I asked for the second time, still texting. She walked up and snatched my phone.

"Motherfucker, you texting my sister? You been threatening her for pussy!" she screamed, throwing my phone at me.

I jumped up, but before I could reach her, she shifted into a large light brown wolf and tackled me. She clawed my chest and went for my neck with her teeth, but I dodged her and shifted into my beast form. We jumped at each other in midair and collided, but she was no match for me. I slammed her through the glass table and ripped her throat open. She was gone. Slowly, her body shifted back to human form. Damn, I never meant to kill her. I just wanted her to be obedient and do what she was supposed to do, and do it right. She couldn't even do that. I ate her, bones and everything. I didn't need this getting out before I had the chance to kill Mega.

I HIT UP DAME, and he agreed to meet me at a bar in Bellmont after a little convincing. I sat in my dark tinted Tahoe in the parking lot of Elixirs. I'd gotten there early so I could survey the area. I waited for about twenty minutes before a black Lexus coupe pulled in and parked a few spaces down from me. Dame stepped out and pulled his pants up on his waist. I didn't miss the gun that was tucked in his back. I watched him give dap to a few niggas outside before he walked in. I didn't feel completely comfortable meeting him here, seeing as this was his turf, but he wouldn't meet anywhere else. Grabbing the book bag off the passenger seat, I stepped out and headed for the door. Dudes gave me funny looks because I wasn't a familiar face, and the women had lust in their eyes. I fucked the human females from time to time, but I'd never mark them. I walked in and looked around at the small bar bathed in a soft green light and cute waitresses. I took note of a few booths off to the left. Dame sat at the last one, staring a hole through me. If looks could kill, I would've been laid out on the floor.

I hoisted the book bag up on my shoulder and made my way to his table. Once I sat, we grilled each other for a moment.

"Fuck you wanted to meet for?" he finally asked.

"First, here's your bread back from the traps I robbed. All three-hundred thousand of it," I said, handing him the book bag over the table. He snatched it, but didn't open it. He never took his eyes off me.

"What's to stop me from killing you now, fuck nigga?" he asked calmly.

I clenched my jaw, trying to keep my anger in check. "Because we need each other's help." I leaned back into my seat.

His face crumpled in confusion. "Fuck I need your help with?" he spat.

I smiled, "You want your bitch back or nah?"

He jumped up and reached behind him. I quickly held my hands up in surrender and shook my head, "Nah, it ain't like that. Yo' bitch is fucking with a nigga that got something that belongs to me. This nigga got clout, so I need help taking him down. The witch with the dreads, that's your bitch, right?"

"What you mean she fucking with him?" he asked.

I could see the heat coming from his head. These sucka for love ass niggas. I was 'bout to gut punch this dumb ass. I nodded my head, "I had my man following this nigga, see if we could catch him slip-ping. He picked up your bitch a couple nights ago, and they went and parked. My man said the nigga was beating the pussy out the frame and he would have just popped him then, but he knew the chick he was with was a witch and he ain't want her pulling no hocus pocus shit, so he fell back," I lied with a straight face.

Just like I thought, it looked like this nigga's soul had left his body.

"You sure it was her?" he yelled.

"My man, ain't too many chicks walking around looking like her."

He sat down defeated. His eyes narrowed and he gritted his teeth. "What you planning?"

14

MEGA

*W*e had two days before Siren and her girl moved into the new house. I knew something was going down between Green River and Bellmont. I knew it when I caught flashes of Siren talking to Drew, who was Bear's right-hand man. What the fuck was he doing in Bellmont? And right near Siren's building? What I was glad for was that since I'm the alpha of alphas, I have more strength and powers than the others. I had the ability to block Siren from my mind when I wanted to, although she couldn't block me from hers. I know she would hit me with question after question if she could read my thoughts at all times, which was understandable with her being a new shifter and just learning about the true capability of her powers. I wanted to keep her as uninvolved as possible, seeing as how she was just becoming comfortable with shifting. I camped out in front of Sirens building daily, hidden behind tints, but I hadn't smelled or seen Drew since his last interaction with Siren. I had a feeling he was hiding. That's why I was in Green River right now with July and Reese, two members of my pack, sniffing around Bear's house. I spotted a few neighbors watching from their windows, but they knew better than to get involved. They knew if I was making a house call, shit was serious. Bear's smell was faint, like he hadn't been home in days. "I hate this niggas smell! Shit smell stale as fuck," July spat, sneezing. I chuckled at him.

July was from one of my packs in Chicago. He named himself July 'cause he always said he was a hot nigga. He was husky and shorter than me; he was a clown, but he handled his business. Reese was his opposite, tall and lean-muscled. Reese was July's alpha, and he was quiet and deadly. He mostly communicated through facial expressions and head nods, but don't be fooled; he was a killer, and his loyalty was to me and his pack. I sniffed again as we got closer to the back door and froze. I smelled a kill. Maybe a few days old. Reese smelled it too. He glanced at July, and he kicked in the door. I walked in after July and took notice of the trashed kitchen and dining room. The smashed table caught my attention; although it was clean, I could tell that a body was here. A shifter. If I'm not mistaken, a female shifter.

"I think he killed his mate," I said. Reese's eyes widened, and July shook his head.

"He killed his wife! That's foul as shit! No disrespect, boss, but why is this dumb motherfucker even in charge of a pack?" July asked.

"I killed his father, who was the alpha at the time. It should have been Bear's brother, but he died before he could take his place, so Bear stepped up. I allowed it only because his father died at my hands, but I think it's time for Bear to join his father in the afterlife."

When I caught up with this bastard I was going to snap his neck, no questions asked. I checked the rest of the house to see if I could find anything, but nothing jumped out at me, which pissed me off even more. I sat down for a minute to clear my head and decided to check on Siren. I eased into her mind, undetected, and saw her laughing with some nigga. I was already hot, but now I was boiling! He was tall and caramel-skinned with long, brown dreads and a fresh shape up. I got the feeling he was a shifter as well. I allowed my anger to seep into her.

"Yo, you playing a real dangerous game," I thought to her.

"Mega, what's wrong?"

"Who is this fuck boy face you all smiling in?"

"Are you jealous, baby? I read this book that said shifters had open relationships."

"WHAT THE FUCK KINDA GAMES YOU PLAYING?" I roared in her head.

"Mega! Stop it! It's my brother. I was just playing with you."

"Y'all fuckin' chicks always calling somebody yo' brother."

"Man, this is my real brother! We both slid out of Willow's cooch!" she laughed.

"You think that shit funny?"

"That's what the fuck you get for pushing me out that tree last night. Then you had the nerve to laugh 'cause I flapped my arms!"

I thought about it. When I pushed her, she was supposed to shift and hit the ground on four paws, not turn into a giant bird. I laughed again.

"See?'"

"You right, but Imma fuck you up when I see you."

She started to say something else, but I tuned her ass out. I swear, she purposely did shit so she could get her pussy pounded on.

WE WALKED around the shifter community, until I picked up his scent again. It was light, but he had been here within the past few days. Walking up to the small house, I kicked in the door, not bothering to knock. A brown-skinned woman with large brown eyes and straight black hair that framed her pretty face jumped to her feet. When she saw me, she dropped to her knees and began crying uncontrollably.

"Please don't kill him!" she begged.

"Where is he?" I asked her, while prying her off my leg.

"Please, Mega! He didn't want to. Bear made him! He blackmailed him!"

I leaned down and sniffed her. Drew. This was Drew's mate. "Where the fuck are they!?" I yelled, gripping her up by her arms and lifting her in the air.

I hated having to manhandle women, but I would if I had to. "I-I don't know where Bear is."

"WHY THE FUCK IS HIS SCENT HERE?!" I roared.

I was getting tired of playing these games. She began crying and shaking, and piss ran down her leg. I let her go.

"Listen, I'm trying not to hurt you, but obviously you know something. Tell me what I want to know or I will end your life," I told her, rubbing my temples.

I could feel my body temperature rising and I wanted to shift and go on a fucking rampage, but if I did, I would wipe everything out. It was always in everyone's best interest that I kept my anger in check, so for the life of me, I was trying to remain cool. As if Reese could read my mind, he patted my shoulder. I stepped back to let him handle it before I nutted up.

"Yo shorty, we know the nigga was here. If you protecting him, that means you got something to do with this shit. Which means the wrath that he gon' feel, you gonna feel it too. You understand?" She shook her head.

"Bear is mated to my sister, but he would come over and... and force me to do sexual things to him. He did that knowing I was mated with Drew." She cried harder. "He had Drew go over to Bellmont to spy on some guys. The Black Cartel, but something happened. I don't know, but Drew said he was coming home, and Bear said he would kill me if he didn't finish the job. I don't know what it is, but it has something to do with you," she said, looking at me.

I watched her as her body shook from fear. I couldn't even be mad at her. This nigga had been torturing her. Shit, he had been torturing his whole pack. I always had my suspicions about Bear, but whenever I came through, the pack never complained about him. They never expressed love, but they never expressed fear and hate either. I was pissed he had his own pack living like this.

"Baby girl, go clean yourself up," I said, glancing at her soaked jeans.

Slowly, she stood and dropped her head as she walked past us on her way to the restroom. "Yooo, what the fuck is going on around here? This nigga around here raping his man's girl?" July said in disbelief.

"We splitting up. I want that motherfucker found tonight! Y'all go check around Bellmont for him or that nigga Drew. Only kill them if you have to. I want those niggas brought to me alive," I said.

They nodded and headed out the door. After about twenty minutes, the woman emerged from the restroom wearing a tiny robe. She did a quick glance around and then dropped her head once she spotted me leaning against the wall. "What's your name?" I asked her.

"Maya," she said in a quiet voice.

"Maya, does Drew know Bear been raping you?" I asked. She shook her head.

"I'm afraid he won't want me anymore if he finds out; besides, Drew is a beta, there's nothing he could do anyway... Mega, would you protect me?" she begged, walking over and throwing herself into my chest.

Quickly, I pushed her off. "I'm already mated," I told her.

"Bear had sex outside of his mate," she said, rubbing my dick through my jeans.

I pushed her harder this time, causing her to fly back into the wall. "Don't ever compare me to that nigga! I have a direct link to the gods and I run shit how they ask me to. Besides, I actually love my mate, and I can still smell piss on you," I told her. She put her head down in embarrassment. I didn't care; I was sick of playing with this girl, and she was right to be embarrassed. Trying to throw her pissy pussy at somebody.

Shaking my head, I snatched her phone off the table and scrolled through her call log, looking for Drew's number. Finding what I was looking for, I pressed the call button. It rang twice before he answered.

"You ok, My?" he asked. I was silent, just listening to any background noises that might give me a clue as to where he was at. It was silent.

"My?" he said.

"Mega, I didn't want anything to do with this. That nigga Bear gone crazy!" he said once he realized it was me and not Maya on the line.

"Where are you, Drew?" I growled lowly into the phone.

"Mega, man please, don't hurt Maya. She ain't have nothing to do with this!"

"Nigga, did I say I hurt her?" I asked.

He breathed a sigh of relief. "Drew, if I go to war with Bear, what side does your allegiance belong to?" I asked him, hoping he gave me the right answer so I wouldn't have to kill him and his mate.

"Yours, Mega. When Bear first sent me over here, it was only to weaken these nigga's team. They was trying to take over Green River, so I was down. But then, he changed up the plan and wanted to go after you. I told that nigga I was out, and he threatened Maya."

I nodded my head, even though he couldn't see me. "Tell me where Bear is," I said.

"Man, I don't know! He only contacts me once a day from an unknown number, and he won't tell me the full plan. Nigga is paranoid. I'm telling you, he gon' crazy," he exhaled loudly.

"Mega, I'll meet you wherever you want so you can look me in my eyes and see I'm not lying. I got nothing but respect for you, and all I want is peace and safety for me and my girl." I didn't speak for a minute because I couldn't promise him that he would be safe.

I wouldn't kill him, but he had to be dealt with for his betrayal. Fuck I look like letting that shit slide?If I let these niggas walk after trying to have me lined up without any repercussions, I was always going to get tried. I realized my mistake was letting Bear walk off with a broken jaw. I should've killed him then. I rattled off an address for him to meet me at and hung up. I glanced at Maya, trying to figure out what I was going to do about her.

15

DAME

$\mathcal{I}$ didn't trust this nigga Bear, which is why I had my brother, Marsean, follow that nigga after he left the bar. He was staying in some rundown motel in East Bellmont, about fifteen minutes from the projects. I felt more at ease knowing we had eyes on him. My next concern was Siren. I had been watching her to see if there was any truth to that fuck nigga's claim. I'd be damned if a couple nights ago, I didn't catch her coming out of her building with this big ass nigga, looking like Idris from *Takers*. I assumed this giant motherfucker was a shifter since I knew the bull Bear was one. They were real familiar with each other, the way this nigga was kissing on her neck and feeling on that lush body that was supposed to be on reserve for me. That hoe had the nerve to look like she was enjoying it too. Man listen, I can't even front. A nigga was hurt when he seen that. I mean, I know I did my dirt but damn, you don't get a nigga back like that.

My heart sank as I realized maybe Bear was telling the truth. I felt like a sucka, watching this dude caress on my girl, and my first instinct was to get out blazing these silver bullets, but then I thought, why not set these niggas up and let them kill each other? That way, I could gain control of Green River since I had a feeling this was the real nigga that ran Green River. He was pushing a Porsche with blacked out windows. Fake Idris wouldn't be in my way, so I could get Siren back. I wondered if she still had her powers. Even if she didn't, shit still worked out for me 'cause now, I could finally fuck. I wasn't worried about if she still wanted a nigga. She was petty, not stupid. Two birds, one bullet, or however the fuck that saying go. All around the board, shit was gonna work out for me. Fuck that, somebody should have told these fuck niggas that you can't hustle a hustler.

I just needed to get these niggas in the same place at the same time, but keep Siren away. If she still had her powers, there was no doubt she would ride for this dark tower ass nigga. It was one in the morning and I was sitting outside her crib, and I hadn't spotted anyone coming or going into the building, so I knew she was by herself. I guess that nigga decided to take a break from digging in the pussy that was supposed to be mine. The more I thought about it, the hotter I got. Shaking my head, I stepped out of my money green Benz with mirror tint and looked around. I was glad to see a few of my niggas back out. Bear informed me he had some of his crew making my team disappear, but now that he thought we were on the same team, he had called them off. It was time for me to start recruiting new hittas. I called one of them over and he hurriedly crossed the street and gave me dap.

"What's up, my nigga. How ya' day go?" I asked the young guy in front of me.

He nodded his head, "It's been steady. Don't worry about nothing, we gon' get it back poppin'," he said, rubbing his hands together.

He was eager and ready to work. I liked him. Maybe I would move him off the corner and give him the trap house Jordan used to run before he went missing. It couldn't hurt to have extra eyes on Siren as well. "What's your name again?" I asked him.

"Cyrus," he replied.

I nodded my head. "Cyrus, I need you to do me a favor. I need you to keep an eye on this building," I said, nodding my head toward Siren's direction, "I wanna know everybody that comes and goes. Especially the girl with the dreads—"

His eyes widened, "I already seen her. That's you?" he asked.

"Yeah. But you know how bitches be on some petty shit. Just keep an eye on her for me."

"No doubt! I got you! I ain't seen her today, but I know that's her truck right there," he said, pointing at the Benz truck I bought her ass.

I spent money like it was nothing when it came to Siren. She was fine as fuck, loyal, for the most part, and her head was fire. She helped the team get dough and she loved a nigga, so I didn't mind breaking bread for her. These other bitches couldn't get a grape soda from me. That's what I needed her to see. She was above these bitches.

"Good looking, homie," I said, dipping off and making my way inside the building. I took my time walking up the stairs because I had no idea what I wanted to say.

By the time I reached her door, I had decided that I would just keep it a hundred with her, which was something that I hadn't always done in the past. Standing still, I listened to see if I could hear any voices or movement on the other side of her door. All I could hear were the loud voices coming from those damn reality shows she watched. I took a deep breath and raised my fist to knock. Before I could connect with the door, she opened it. I smiled inside because I knew she still had her powers, so maybe there was a chance she didn't fuck homie. I ignored the look of annoyance on her face and glanced at the rest of her body. Even with her freshly washed face, dreads pulled up into a messy bun and an oversized tee shirt, she was still one of the most gorgeous women I'd ever seen.

"Damian, I'm really not feeling well, so if you came here to lie some more, fight—" she started, but I held up my hand and shook my head to silence her.

"I didn't come here on no bullshit, I promise. I just need to talk to you," I spoke calmly.

She stared at me for a moment, contemplating. Finally, she stepped to the side and allowed me in. Once inside, I looked around and noticed half of her shit was packed. Damn, she was really done with a nigga. She was gonna bounce without even a bye. I turned to look at her, and she held my gaze for a few seconds before dropping her head, reminding me of the first time I realized I really loved her. The night she was naked in my bathroom. I moved toward her, filling in the few feet that stood between us and lifted her chin, forcing her to look at me.

"Don't do that. I did this. I fucked shit up, man," I said softly, patting my chest so she would know that I wasn't angry with her. Grabbing her hand, I led her to the couch and waited for her to sit before I did. Sitting forward, I placed my head in my hands.

"You moving?" I asked, already knowing the answer.

"Yeah... I just think it's time for a new beginning, you know?" she said in a sad voice.

Nodding my head, I had to put a nail in my own coffin, so I turned to her and asked, "With your new nigga?"

Biting her bottom lip, she nodded her head. I fell back on the couch, like the force from her simple head nod had knocked the wind from my body.

Sighing, I spoke. "Listen Siren, I know I hurt you a lot. I know you put up with a lot. I did a lot of foul ass shit. Kayla's baby is probably mine, but I want you to know that I loved you. I still do... I just had a fucked-up way of showing it. I never regretted loving you, I regret that I didn't know how to love you. I was selfish as fuck and if I could do this shit over, I swear on my mama I would do shit right." I paused 'cause there was this weird feeling in my chest, like I was about to have a heart attack or something.

I breathed deeply until the pain passed, then I glanced at Siren, who had her head on the armrest of the couch. I could tell by the way her body was shaking that she was silently crying. I pulled her onto my chest where she sobbed, wetting my shirt. I used my thumb to wipe her tears.

"Are you happy with this new nigga?" I asked. She nodded her head against my chest.

"I am," she whispered. There was that fucking feeling in my chest again; this time, I tried to breathe through my mouth to relieve it, but something wet ran down my face. I looked up to see if she had a leak in her ceiling. I couldn't spot one, but my vision was becoming blurry. I know good and goddamn well I was not in here laying my cards on the table and she was putting some type of spell on me. I moved her off my chest and jumped up. I felt weird as shit. She stared at me with large watery eyes before she spoke.

"Dame, are... are you crying!?"

"WHAT? Hell no. Did you put some kind of root on me?" I yelled as more water ran down my face.

She shook her head profusely. "I swear I didn't! I... I didn't know you could cry," she said.

"Nigga, I can't. It's probably sweat. Why you ain't got the air on?" I questioned, wiping my face with the back of my arm.

She jumped up and stood in front of me, studying my face, "So, you sweating from your eyes?" she quizzed.

I thought about it. I had never cried before. I had seen other people cry, but... I touched the corner of my eye as more of the liquid poured out.

"Nigga, is these tears?" I asked, confused.

Siren fell onto the couch laughing while I stood there confused. I ran to her bathroom and looked in the mirror. Sure enough, my watery eyes were rimmed in red, and I actually watched a shiny tear slide out of my eye, down my cheek, and get lost in my beard. My nose was even running a little. Quickly, I turned on the cold water and splashed my face until I felt like a nigga again. I turned to see Siren had walked up.

"You okay?" she asked. I paused, 'cause my head was all fucked up.

Letting out a deep breath, I said, "Nah, I'm not okay. I'm fucked up behind this, but I want you to be happy and if I ain't the nigga to make you happy, then I gotta be man enough to step to the side."

She started that crying shit again. "Thank you for this, Dame," she said, reaching up to touch my face. "I never regretted loving you either."

I knew she was about to hit me with some we'll always be friends bullshit, so before she could, I kissed her. I poured every ounce of emotion I had into that kiss, and she didn't stop me. I kissed her until

I felt her legs go weak, and then I leaned her against the door and slowly backed off.

I knew I would probably never get that chance again, so I went for it. If she would have slapped me, it still would have been worth it.

I ran my hand down the side of her face. "Don't be a stranger, Siren," I said, because I didn't want to say bye.

She nodded her head and kept her body pressed against the bathroom door as I made my way out of her crib. I needed to get to the loud I had stashed in my car ASAP! On my way to the car, I bumped into Cyrus again.

"Aye boss man, you check on your chick?" he asked.

"Yeah, but um, listen... I don't need you to report back to me every tit for tat she do. She won't be here much longer, but while she's here, just make sure she's safe. I mean, if you think she's in danger, don't hesitate to lay a nigga down, you feel me?" I said.

"Say no more," he said, giving me dap. Sliding into my Benz, I immediately opened the hidden compartment under the driver's seat and grabbed my pre-rolled blunt. Sparking it, I inhaled the pungent smoke and leaned back into my tan leather. I knew I had to reset my plan. I had to take out that nigga Bear. I couldn't risk him hurting Siren. I grabbed my phone to holla at Marsean and to let him know the new game plan.

16

BEAR

I was laying low in this dingy motel, but it was worth it as my plan was coming together brilliantly. I had Drew tailing Siren, reporting to me all her movements. He was the weakest link between him and Dame, so I decided to keep my whereabouts hidden from him. I didn't trust him enough to know where I laid my head now. I still was able to get to a dollar since I had my niggas in Green River still hustling. I couldn't complain, shit was sweet and in the next couple of days, I would be king. While I was waiting for my daily report from Drew, I decided to go pick up one of these hoes that frequented these types of establishments. The swelling in my jaw was completely gone; my shit had healed and tightened faster than bitches' pussies after they give birth. I ran some water in my hands and rubbed it through my hair, which was curly on top and faded close on the sides with a long chin strap that framed my face. I threw on some large, black shades, even though it wasn't sunny out and left out of my room. This was my first time noticing a bar across the street. It almost looked out of place, seeing as there was nothing else around. It was a tiny, hole-in-the-wall dive bar, but I knew I could get some Henny up in me and find some easy pussy.

Throwing open the rusty metal door, I walked in and stopped in my tracks. It was larger inside than the outside let on. There was a small stage in the center of the floor, with an actual stripper putting on a show to Rihanna's "Pour it Up." Most of the crowd was occupying space in front of the stage, although there were a few stragglers at the bar. Most of the people in here were old men who looked like they had a rough life. And fuck them old, dusty hookers I'd seen around the area, I was gonna bag a stripper! I sat at one of the empty, worn barstools and signaled the bartender, who was this big burly guy with slicked back, greasy hair. I ordered never-ending cups of Henny straight and watched the dancer on stage. By the time I was on my fourth cup, I noticed the lights dim, and heard the beginning chords of Trey Songz "All We Do." I swiveled my stool around to face the stage as I downed my cup. I watched this girl slowly make her way onto the stage. She wore giant heeled shoes, black leather shorts, with a matching black leather bustier. She was toned and curvy. She had the face of an angel with a short, spiky pixie cut. Her hair was so red it almost looked orange, giving her innocent face a devilish undertone. Her flawless skin was reddish brown, like cinnamon.

The flashing lights made the red and gold glitter all over her oiled body sparkle. I, along with everyone else, was hypnotized as she started to wind her body to the rhythm.

'I ain't trying to stop and I know she with it,
I can see it in her eyes she been down from the beginning,
And she can't leave me alone cause I drive her body crazy,
I done gave her a little taste now she want to have my babies.'

AT THAT POINT, she climbed up the pole and slid down into a split, gyrating her pussy on the ground. Leaning over, she ran her hands down her legs and back up, suddenly ripping her top off, revealing firm, large breasts with little metal bars piercing through her burgundy nipples. I maneuvered my way through the crowd until I was right up against the stage. I had to see her up close. She leaned back, propping her legs against the pole as she gripped her breasts while looking at me upside down. I drizzled a few dollars over her stomach and she grinned and spread her legs, lifting her ass and sliding off the shorts. She was now only wearing heels and a thin red thong. She flipped over so that she was on her hands and knees and began to slowly twerk her plump ass in my face. I sniffed her pussy, and my dick instantly bricked up. I could see through the thin material of her panties that her clit was pierced. That shit was so sexy. I loved when a bitch liked a little pain. She stood and faced me with her pussy directly in my face, so close that if I would've stuck out my tongue, I would've tasted her. She fascinated the crowd with more acrobatic tricks until her time was up. As she bent to scoop up her money, I waited until she was directly in front of me before I spoke.

"I want a private dance," I told her. Lifting her head, she looked me up and down, finally staring at me with her large brown eyes.

A slow smile crept on her face before she asked, "Can you afford it?" Her voice sounded like water running softly over rocks and I was momentarily in a trance, watching her full lips move. Nodding my head, I held up a wad of money. Her eyes lit up. "Let me go freshen up, and I'll meet you right in there," she said, pointing to a door that I hadn't noticed before.

It was off in the corner. I nodded, but stood there watching her titties slightly bounce as she collected the rest of her money. Once she walked back through the velvet curtain, I headed over to the door she instructed me to. Upon entering, faint rhythmic music played. It sounded foreign, with low drum beats, violins, and bells. As I walked down the small hallway, moans and groans of pleasure could be heard behind the curtains that partitioned off little rooms. I found an empty one and walked in. There was only enough room for one small, soft-looking couch inside. Before I could sit down, the smell of night jasmine invaded my nostrils. Turning around, I saw her standing there in a simple black silk robe, loosely tied, allowing large portions of her flawless bare skin to peek through. I didn't think it was possible for me to get any harder, but I did. It was almost painful.

I handed her the entire roll of money. Without counting it, she opened a drawer inside of the wall that I hadn't noticed before and tossed it in.

"What's your name?" she asked.

"Bear," I said, and she raised a perfectly arched brow and glanced at my dick print through my pants.

"I'm Jade," she said, placing her hand on my chest and lightly pushing me back until I sat down on the couch.

She climbed onto my lap and began rubbing her body over me, never breaking eye contact. After I got tired of her teasing, I opened her silky robe all the way and slipped it off her shoulders. Running my hands all over her glorious body, I pressed her down on my erection while she threw her head back and let out a light, throaty laugh, sending vibrations straight to my dick. She began winding her body down on me as I fondled her large breasts, becoming irritated that these jeans were in my way of what I just knew was some good pussy. As if she could sense my agitation, she leaned forward and whispered in my ear, "You want more?"

Without answering her, I grabbed her hips and lifted her in the air until her legs were resting on my shoulders and her pussy was in my face. I dove in, hungrily attacking her clit.

"Ohhhh!" she said with a light giggle. I sucked and lapped at her while she ground against my tongue.

Quickly, I felt her shudder and her sweet juices poured into my mouth, dripping down my chin. I kept going, using one hand to hold her up and with the other, I unzipped my jeans and pulled my dick out. Lowering her down from my face, I began easing her onto me. I watched her large eyes become wider as the tip of my dick stretched her open. She started to lift herself up, but I slammed her down until I was buried in her.

"Uhhh!" I grunted, and she moaned in my ear as she started to ride me. Her pussy was tight and wet and she was clutching my shit, causing my toes to curl.

She was leaking all over me as she screamed and picked up her pace. My nut was close, so I pressed her into my chest and pumped into her until I released, but I was still hard. I started to feel weak, but I needed more. Standing, I lifted her up while still hard inside of her and dropped her on the couch. I pounded into her like a mad man. The wet, squishy sounds her pussy was making were driving me crazy. I felt another nut building and her pussy was sucking me in deeper every time I stroked into her.

"Ahhhhhhhhhh!" My whole body tingled as I busted inside her, but I was still hard. I was starting to feel dizzy and it was hard for me to catch my breath, so I stumbled back.

Jade pushed me down, hopped her sweaty body back on my dick and began riding me like her life depended on it. I was screaming like a bitch as my body parts began stiffening up, but this pussy still felt amazing. When she pressed her soft lips to mine, it was like she was sucking the breath out of my body. Succubus.

"Stop!" I roared, trying to push her off me, but I was weakened and she was still throwing that pussy on me.

She pouted. "No, daddy. I wanna cum too," she said, planting her feet on the ground and twerking on me. "Ohhhh, yeah!" she moaned.

I felt another nut coming on and it felt incredible. I sucked her nipple into my mouth. "Ummmmm," she moaned on top of me.

I knew I had to stop before this bitch killed me and collected my soul. I mustered all the strength I had and pushed her off me, scrambling to my feet. Breathing hard with shaky hands, I tried to tuck my still hard dick back into my jeans, but before I could, she was on me again; this time, forcing my dick into her mouth.

"Ahhh, FUCK!!" I yelled as pleasure shot through my body and I gripped the back of her head. I pushed myself deeper into her throat as she slurped me up. I gathered the little strength I had and punched her in her face and ran out of the room. Dick still out and everything, I was running out of the bar. I stumbled back across the street and entered my room, collapsing on the floor.

∾

I COULD HEAR faint voices as I started to come to. It sounded like laughter.

"I really think this nigga on drugs. He stumbled across the street with his dick out, bro!" a deep voice said.

More laughter. I was struggling to wake up; I had to be dreaming. I felt cold metal nudge my temple. "Aye, wake yo bitch ass up, nigga!" My eyes shot open, but I still only saw pitch black. I heard Jade's throaty laugh and I tried to jump up, but I hit my head on the cold metal.

As I came out of my daze, I was dizzy as hell, but I could make out two male figures. I tried to shift; it was painful, but I could do it. Just as my claws and teeth extended... POW! I felt fire pierce my leg.

"NIGGA, FUCK OUTTA HERE WITH THAT TEEN WOLF SHIT. I GOT THIS HOT SILVER FOR YOUR ASS." I could make out Dame's voice.

I grabbed my leg, trying to stop the fire from spreading, "End this shit and stop playing with the nigga," the other one, who I assumed was his brother, said.

Dame looked in his direction, and I took that split second to leap on him. I sunk my teeth into Dame and slammed him into the wall. He shot two bullets into my stomach before he crumpled to the floor.

"DAME!!!" his brother screamed before unloading bullets of his own.

I was dodging most but caught one in my arm and chest. Fuck, I was losing blood fast.

When he ran out of bullets, I grabbed him and tossed him into a wall, then ran out as fast as I could. My body was on fire. I knew if I could get to Mega, I could kill him and use his blood to rejuvenate. I was damn near in and out of consciousness from the pain that felt like it was engulfing my body, but still, I managed to make it to Bellmont Projects, where I threw my truck into park in the middle of the street, left the keys in the ignition, and jumped out as fast as my battered body would let me.

I knew if I didn't get to Mega soon, I was going to die from these wounds. Sniffing the air, I caught a whiff of Drew's scent and also

Mega, but it was infused with something sweet and I knew it was his bitch. My nigga Drew came through. She was in the woods. Once I had her, it would be easy as fuck to get to Mega. I took off running toward the woods at full speed, shifting along the way. I wasn't as fast or as strong as I normally was, but I knew I could still take her, heal up for a couple days, and then end Mega.

17

SIREN

"The advantage I have is that he doesn't know I'm a shifter," I said to Mega, my brother Reese, and July, who all sat directly in front of me.

Drew and his girlfriend, Maya, sat off to the right, silent aside from their low murmurs to each other now and then. Gee sat to the left, staring at everyone with wide eyes. Mega shook his head, but of course, my brother spoke first.

"You must've lost your mind! Ain't nobody using you as bait!" he yelled.

"Using me as bait is the only way to trap him. If he smells Mega, he won't come. If he smells you niggas..." I paused, pointing at Mike, Reese, and July. "He'll know it's an ambush. He has to smell Drew and me!" I yelled back, throwing my arms in the air.

We went back and forth like this for about an hour until they finally, reluctantly agreed with me when they realized no other way would work. I did agree to take Mike with me since he was a half blood, like me; his smell could easily be covered. I had a headache! I was really sitting around arguing with these stubborn assholes. I was even arguing with niggas' facial expressions since, apparently, Reese didn't talk. We were in my apartment, which was pretty much void of furniture since we were moving tomorrow. I wanted to dead this shit before I moved into the new house. There was no way I planned on dragging this ghetto shit with me to North Bellmont. I was gonna be bad and bougie, lounging around my pool!

"Drew, did he respond yet?" I gritted while asking him. I wanted to kill his ass for setting me up in the first place. Sending that crazy nigga pictures of me and shit. His nose was broken where Mega had socked him, but I thought that was letting him off to easy. I wasn't supposed to publicly question my alpha, but he would definitely hear about it the minute we were alone. I didn't like his bitch at all. She kept eyeing me whenever she thought I wasn't looking. I was about three seconds from dragging her.

Drew checked his phone. "No. I sent him the message that I had you about an hour ago." I rolled my eyes.

Weak excuse from a weak nigga. The Maya bitch sucked her teeth. "It's not his fault Bear didn't respond yet," she said smartly.

I let out a low growl before I leapt on her, knocking her to the ground. I was raining blow after blow, unleashing all my anxiety and pent up frustration on her until my fist was covered in blood.

"DREW, GET THIS CRAZY BITCH OFF ME!" she screamed.

Drew didn't move, but Mega grabbed me and lifted me in the air, kicking and screaming.

"Bitch, I should kill you!" she yelled at me as if she hadn't learned her lesson while wiping blood out of her eye.

Before I knew it, Gee had jumped out of her seat and tackled Maya to the ground. They were rolling around, but Gee was getting the best of her. I rooted her on and managed to wiggle out of Mega's grasp. I hopped on that bitch again, and me and Gee took turns fucking her up until Mega grabbed me again; Mike and Reese grabbed Gee while July laughed.

"Let them fight! This better than *Monday Night Raw*! Yooo, how your bitch get her ass kicked by a human? You better get her some fighting lessons," he said to Drew, still laughing.

"Nobody talks shit to my best friend, but me!" Gee said, smoothing the back of her hair down.

"That's right, best friend!" I said. We cheered each other on and shouted how much we loved each other while Maya cowered in the corner, and the guys looked at us like we were crazy.

I walked into the kitchen to get bottled waters for me and Gee while Mega followed behind me.

"You ok?" Mega asked, raising a brow. I made sure to flash images of the new house in my mind in case he tried to invade my thoughts. Yeah, I couldn't block him but with a little will power, he would only see what I wanted him to see.

These past few days, I couldn't help thinking of Dame. Take today, for instance. Once Dame would've got the info he needed from Drew, he would've murdered him and his tired looking girlfriend and not had them sitting in my living room breathing my gotdamn air. I know Mega had all these rules and a correct way of doing shit and blah blah blah, but I was used to Dame, who ran off passion and emotion. I know... I wasn't shit for standing here comparing the two... but... that kiss I shared with Dame had me shook because it was pure. I felt everything about him as though I temporarily invaded his soul. I know I wasn't shit for allowing him to kiss me like that, but trust me, I wasn't gonna let it happen again. I had a good dude, who didn't cheat on me and get random hoes pregnant, and I planned on keeping him. But still, I needed that closure from Dame. Besides, even if I did want Damian, I couldn't have him. Remember, we had that whole star-crossed lovers thing going on? I focused my attention on the handsome, but worried man in front of me.

"Why are they still alive?" I asked, trying to keep my voice down. Mega rubbed his hand through his skillfully lined goatee.

"Because, I want to make sure all the info that Drew gave is factual. Once everything is settled, he'll be punished accordingly."

"What about Maya?"

"Bear raped her and killed her sister, that's a tougher situation," he said.

I wasn't satisfied with his explanations, so instead of responding, I simply stared at him.

"You sure that's the only thing bothering you?" he asked, staring at me.

I let out a sigh. "Yeah, I'm just frustrated with all this shit," I said, motioning toward the living room, "Then, the move tomorrow, and you know I haven't been feeling well." I said.

"I know... are you positive you want to go out here tonight? You could just mark the trees." I held up my hand to stop him.

"No, I don't want to fuck this up. I want to make sure his ass dies in those woods tonight." Mega nodded his head.

"You know I'll protect you with my last breath." I nodded my head, feeling a little better.

He wrapped me in a tight hug and started kissing my neck, and I smiled into his chest. I felt loved and safe tucked in his embrace. I needed to get thoughts of Dame out of my head and have faith in my man. When he released me, I opened the fridge, grabbed two bottles, and walked back out to hand Gee hers before I plopped down next to her.

"Damn, you ain't bring no water for your other guests?" July said.

I rolled my eyes. He was handsome in a stocky football player kind of way. He was caramel -skinned with curly hair that he wore in a wild fro, but the scar under his eye kept him from being too pretty. That and his deep, scratchy voice. Unscrewing the cap, I took a long sip before I responded.

"Nigga, you wasn't with me shooting in the gym. Take your ass to the river." I joked, causing the room to laugh.

He was always cracking jokes on somebody! Let's see if he could take it.

He nodded his head. "You got that. I'm going outside to get some air," he said, but I really knew he was going out to blow because Mega couldn't stand the smell of loud.

His nose was too sensitive. I started to go out with him; I needed something to calm my nerves, but Gee grabbed my wrist. "We need to talk," she whispered.

I nodded toward the bedroom 'cause it was the only space not occupied by this fake ass task force. Once inside, she closed the door. "Okay bitch, are you pregnant?" she asked with a hand on her hip.

My eyes ballooned so wide I knew I probably looked comical. "What? No! Why would you ask me that?" I spat.

She studied my face and body before speaking. "You haven't been feeling well, your hips and breasts are spreading, and you've been in your feelings heavy." I looked down at my boobs in the black crop top I was wearing.

It had the word 'witch' stitched on it in white letters going across my chest, and the letters were stretched to maximum capacity. Fuck. And I had been overly emotional lately. What if she was right?

"Is it too early for a pregnancy test?" I asked her.

"I don't know, but..." she paused, digging in her bag, "I got an extra one here. Take after first missed period," she read off the box.

I frowned my face up as she handed it to me and looked her nasty ass up and down. Her ass was good for pulling condoms, lube and now, apparently pregnancy tests out of those giant bags she rocked.

"Don't judge me, hoe!" she yelled.

I cracked up laughing and soon, she joined me. I made sure to hide the test under my pillow before we walked back out, planning on taking it later. I didn't have time to process this new information, because just as we exited the bedroom, July came barging in the front door sneezing.

"That nigga close! I smell his stale ass scent!" he yelled.

Mega snatched Drew up. "Drew, Mike, Siren, get to the woods now!" he yelled.

I was already on my way to the window. I paused momentarily and placed my hand on my stomach. "Siren," Mega said. I turned, and he was looking directly at my hand on my stomach. Shit.

"I'm good," I said quickly before jumping out of the window and shifting before I hit the ground with precision. I had gotten good at doing this since Mega liked pushing me out of trees and shit. I heard Drew and Mike do the same behind me, and we took off into the woods.

"Damn! You shift big as shit. Almost as big as me," Mike proclaimed wordlessly while jumping over me and running full speed.

"Fuckin show off," I thought. He was big with long black and gold fur. He laughed and jumped into the trees until he was so camouflaged, even I couldn't see him anymore, but I knew he was there.

I shifted back into human form, rubbed dirt on myself, and sat on the ground, forcing tears out and hoping I looked battered. I noticed Drew staring at my body, but when he saw me watching, he quickly turned his head. He was about my size in his wolf form and dark, chocolate brown fur covered his body. I sucked my teeth and thought about killing him myself, but decided to let Mega handle it. After a few minutes, I could smell the stank scent that July was talking about. I heard footsteps and my heart rate sped up. As the steps grew closer, I looked towards the sounds of them and peered into the darkness. That's when I saw him. He had shifted into human form, a fake ass Christopher Williams from *New Jack City*-looking motherfucker. Boy, that uni brow. He probably thought he was the shit too. He was tall and stocky and he looked hurt; there was blood everywhere, like he had been in a war before getting here.

Drew shifted to human form. "What the fuck happened to you?" he asked.

"That bitch nigga Dame and his brother ambushed me and shot me with silver bullets, trying to stop me from getting to this bitch." He glanced at me. "I made sure I killed that nigga, though." he laughed with this crazed look in his eyes.

What!? I could feel my temperature rising and my stomach started to cramp up as I tried to control my anger.

"What, bitch? You big mad I killed your little side piece?" he said, eyeing my body and stalking toward me. "Might as well get some pussy before I kill yo' other nigga." Before he could get to me, I jumped to my feet, shifted, and charged him.

He tried to shift, but due to his multiple wounds, he wasn't as swift as me. He only managed to extend his claws and fangs before I knocked him down and went for his throat, but he dodged me and I ended up taking a chunk out of his shoulder. I tasted the silver and it stunned me. My mouth was on fire. Fuck the atomic hot sauce they pour over hot wings at the corner store; this shit was like actual fire.

In the moment I was stunned, he pierced me with his claws, ripping into my flesh, and I whimpered in pain. I heard Mike running up. He pushed me out of the way and began tearing into Bear anywhere he could. Within seconds, Mega, Reese and July appeared and joined in. Mega clamped down on his throat, and I heard the bones crunching as it was ripped to shreds.

"Never liked you anyway, pretty motherfucka," July said, quoting Nino while standing over Bear's body.

I laughed until I had tears in my eyes. This nigga was a fool. Slowly, I stood to my feet and shifted back. Mike stared at me with wide eyes.

"Boy, we're shifters. Get used to seeing me naked," I said. He shook his head.

"No, Siren... your stomach," he said.

I looked down and saw the deep gash with blood pouring from the wound and down my legs. With a shaky hand, I ran my fingers through the blood and chunks that were seeping out of my body. I looked up and saw Mega running toward me before I blacked out.

18

DAME

*W*hen I opened my eyes into the pitch black, almost immediately, a musty smell permeated my nose. My hand instantly shot to the left side of my neck. It was sore as fuck. but there was no gash where that fuck nigga bit me. I wondered if I imagined that shit. I heard slight movement off to my right, and then a low groan.

"Marsean!" I yelled.

"Bro, you alive," he said in a weak voice. I sat up and focused my vision toward the direction of his voice. Even though it was pitch black inside the motel room, I could see him clearly. He sat propped up against the wall. Blood ran out of his nose, and there were small cuts all over his face. I stood carefully, but surprisingly, my body felt ok. It felt great, actually, aside from the throbbing pain in my neck. Making my way to Marsean, I surveyed the damage to his body close-up. He was cut and bruised badly, but I didn't see anything that appeared life threatening.

"Can you move?" I asked, squatting down in front of him. I watched as he sat up slowly and stretched his legs.

"I think my back is broke," he said.

"Nigga, if your back was broke, you wouldn't be able to sit up!" I told him.

"Well nigga, I don't know! A fucking wolf slammed me through a wall damn near!" he yelled.

I grabbed his arms and helped him to his feet. I lifted the back of his shirt, and his back was filled with black and purple bruises, but it wasn't broken.

"Can you walk?" I asked. He took one step.

"AHHH, FUCK!" he yelled, backing up against the wall. I scooped him up like he was a feather and headed out to his truck.

"Nigga, how the fuck is you lifting me so easy? And, I heard that nigga chomp through your bones, why the fuck is it just a bruise?" he asked as I carefully placed him in the passenger seat. Touching my neck again, I shrugged my shoulders.

"Man, I don't know. But we gotta get to Siren. I gotta make sure she's not hurt, and then she can do something for your pain."

"Shit, Imma do something for the pain! Look in my glove compartment and spark that weed for me," he said.

I lit the blunt, passed it to him, and sped out, headed for Siren. Something in my gut told me she wasn't okay, but I ignored the feeling and gunned the engine.

I pulled up to her building in record speed! Running around the truck, I grabbed Marsean out and hauled ass up the four flights of stairs, carrying my brother, who was looking at me like I was crazy. Gently, I placed him on his feet outside of her door. I smelled Siren... wait. I could actually smell her sweet musky scent through the door, but I could also smell blood and my heart dropped. I also picked up three or four different male scents.

"Imma kick this motherfucker down, just stay against the wall and keep your hammer pointed at any fuckin' body that gets in the way," I whispered.

I took a deep breath and kicked the door. My foot went through it as the door came completely off the hinges. Marsean slid in quickly, using the wall for leverage with his hammer out and the blunt hanging from his lips. My nigga was a fucking G. I had my gun trained on the first nigga that came running out of the bedroom.

"Where the fuck is Siren?" I roared. I watched this nigga begin to shift. and I quickly cocked my gun. "Motherfucker, I'll fill your ass up with this silver, same way I did Bear!" I yelled, causing him to stop mid shift and cock his head at me.

I had a stare down with this running back nigga until the dude I recognized as Siren's new nigga yelled, "Who the fuck are you!?"

"Nigga, where's Siren!?" I screamed.

"Dame?" I heard her weak voice call from inside the bedroom.

I glanced at Marsean, who gave the head nod for me to go. Keeping my gun aimed at Idris's head, I eased by him into the bedroom. My heart damn near exploded when I saw Siren lying on her bed, her blood making a deep stain around her. I looked at her homie, Gee, who wore a sad expression as she wiped Siren's face with a wet washcloth. I noticed two other niggas in the room, one I recognized as Siren's brother from her Instagram. Nigga was big as shit in person. The other I didn't know, but he looked like a tall Big Sean and was staring daggers at me, so I aimed at him as I walked over to Siren, who was silently watching me through half-opened eyes. I touched her face.

"I tried to stop that nigga, Si, I—" She squeezed my hand to silence me.

"I know," she smiled. "You weakened him and we finished that fuck nigga," she spat.

I smiled because even when she was hurt, she talked more shit than a nigga. My smile dropped as I ran my eyes over her body. "But he got you..." I said, my head hanging down.

Tears ran out of her eyes "Yeah, but I'll live, my baby didn't. though." I was shocked.

Damn, she had went and got herself knocked. I looked behind me at her new nigga, who was staring me down. I hated this nigga. I wish his ass would have gotten murked too.

"So, let me get this straight... your new nigga let that motherfucker close enough to touch you? And you was pregnant?" I screamed.

I could literally feel my blood turn hot, and my nostrils flared as I inhaled deeply. New nigga let out a loud growl and started to shift.

"Stop! Both of you!" Siren yelled. "Dame, it wasn't his fault. The shit happened in like two seconds. We didn't know I was pregnant. I just found out when the spirits came and took him. I'd be dead from hemorrhaging right now if it wasn't for Mega's blood. What the hell happened to you? Bear said he killed you. And, and—" She broke down crying.

I didn't care how many excuses she made; in my mind, her dude was a fuck nigga who allowed his girl and baby to get hurt. If I would have been here with her, that nigga wouldn't have gotten within reaching distance of her. I loved her, and she still loved a nigga. I could tell. This nigga was 'bout to have to go to war with me and he ain't even know it. I don't give a fuck if he a shifter!

"Man, Si, that nigga took a bite out of me like I was dinner and I thought I was dead... but when I woke up, I only had this bruise," I pointed to my neck.

I could see the confusion on her face. "WHAT?" new nigga roared. The other two niggas stared at me in shock.

"Nigga, you a new shifter," the running back bull spoke. Now, I stared at them in shock. Suddenly, the shit made sense. My sense of smell was heightened, I was stronger than normal, night vision. Get the fuck out of here. I was a motherfucking shifter. Just to be sure, I emptied one of the silver bullets out of the chamber and held it in my hand.

"Ahhhhhhhhhhhh!" I yelled as the shit sizzled my skin.

Quickly, I dropped it on the floor and it rolled under Siren's bed. Marsean eased his way into the room, still using the wall as a crutch.

"Y'all niggas done playing detective and shit. This nigga had us on stakeouts, kicking in doors, guns blazing like we auditioning for a new bad boys movie, and y'all talking about shit that I already knew when this nigga lifted me up like I was a fucking bitch. Meanwhile, my fuckin back is broke in about six different places!" Marsean yelled.

The whole room broke out into laughter at this nigga's dramatic ass. Everybody except fake Idris, anyway. Gee, who was still laughing and wiping tears from her eyes, grabbed Siren's salve that was on her nightstand. "Turn around, Sean," she said.

"I can't!" he yelled

"Hold up! Nigga, you busted up in here, waving a gun with a fuckin' blunt hanging from your mouth and you damn near paralyzed?" running back said, causing another round of laughter.

"Fuck y'all niggas!" Marsean gritted.

"Gee, come rub that magical shit on my back."

"Oh nah, nigga! The only motherfucker she rubbin' is me, my nigga!" Siren's brother said, standing up. "Get the chick in the living room to do it," he said, gently tossing my brother over his shoulder and walking out.

I could still hear Marsean's voice. "That chick in the corner that look like a hostage."

I chuckled at him again, then focused back on Siren. "Wait... you was pregnant and still had your powers?" I asked, confused.

She nodded. "Dame... I'm half shifter. My father was a shifter and my mom is a witch. If I have sex with a shifter or male witch, my powers remain intact," she said, not making eye contact with me.

I sat down in the chair near her bed and placed my head in my palms. I jumped up because I accidentally rubbed the raw spot the silver bullet left. So much shit was running through my mind. Outweighing everything was the fact that I had another chance. Another chance with Siren. This time, I would do shit right. I swore on my mama.

"Dame, I'm mated... to Mega," she said, pointing to new nigga and dashing my hopes. I looked at her and saw the love and relief that I wasn't hurt, so I knew I still had a chance because she still cared.

I was going to get her back if it took everything out of me. "Mated?" I said.

She nodded. "Mega is my alpha."

"And yours too," Running back added.

I frowned my face up, "Nigga, that sound gay. Ain't no other nigga my alpha. This ain't no fifty shades of gray shit," I spat.

"Dame! Don't be disrespectful. There are politics and rules shifters must follow," Siren advised.

"The penalty is death," new nigga said, staring a hole in me.

Just then, Marsean walked into the room, shirtless, stretching his arms. All the bruises were gone. "Good looking, Si!" he said. "Come on, Fido! I need some rest after you had me on these navy seal missions. And you bet not get no fleas in my truck," he said, walking out the room.

I looked at Siren, who nodded her head. "I'll be good as new," she assured me.

Leaning over, I lightly sniffed her and enjoyed her smell. When I heard her nigga's bones cracking, Siren's brother placed a hand on his arm and shook his head.

"Y'all handle this later, let my sis have her peace," he said in a low voice, like he didn't wanna anger that nigga.

I stood and walked toward the door, but not before throwing another look to Siren. I was coming back for her and no politics, rules, alphas— whatever was gonna stop me.

19

MEGA

I was glad to have all this shit behind us. I was still hurt behind losing a seed. If I had known, there would have been no way I would have let that woman talk me into putting her in the middle. The second I felt Siren's anger, I was out that window making it to them in seconds, but by the time I got there, Mike was already ripping into Bear. Once I realized Siren was hurt, it was too late. I was able to save her, but the baby was gone almost instantly. I grieved every night for the son I didn't get to meet. Siren made a full recovery, and her scar was no longer visible. We were all moved into our new spot. Mike, who was becoming like a brother to me because he had a lot of his father's qualities, ended up selling his house in LA and moving into the crib with Gee. Reese had left and returned to Chicago, but July opted to stay, so he was living in the house with Siren and I. We were starting to form our own little pack. One thing that still bothered me was that nigga Dame.

I was getting tired of following all these rules, while these little new niggas were disrespectful. I was dangerously close to going renegade and just laying niggas down. Siren filled me in on their history and assured me I had nothing to worry about, but I could tell he wanted what I had, and I couldn't stand that nigga. I was looking for any reason to come at his head. So far, he'd been quiet since he was now alpha of Green River. Another reason why I was growing tired of all these rules. Because Bear had no children but he created Dame, it was law that Dame lay claim to his land. I checked on Green River daily, but the shifters there insisted Dame and his brothers were fair leaders and the community was prospering. So, I had no cause to touch him... yet. I killed Drew in the woods that night after my anger got the best of me when I watched Siren collapse. I saw red, watching her life almost slip away, and I pulled his body apart limb from limb and eventually sent Maya back to Green River.

Today, I had been out hunting in the woods behind our house and was walking through the door with a giant deer slung over my shoulder. Siren was gonna steak me to death. I loved steak, but she could eat that shit every night! So, I went out to catch something different. Walking into the kitchen, I slung the buck onto the table and washed my hands. I needed some pussy. Something about hunting brought out my primal instincts. I stalked through the house, searching for her ass 'cause she was on the menu.

"Oh daddy! I missed you so much!" I heard her say.

Following the sound of her voice, I said. "Daddy missed you too, but I've only been gone an hour." I stopped in my tracks when I saw Siren and her mother kneeled before the giant mirror she had me hang in the hallway.

They were surrounded by a circle of white powder with little symbols everywhere, and they had candles lit. Their heads swiveled to me as I walked up. Her mother, Willow, had a smirk on her face, while Siren looked embarrassed.

"Uh hmm... hello, old friend. It's nice to see you again, but I'm pretty sure MY daughter was talking to me when she said Daddy," a voice I recognized spoke to me from the mirror.

I stepped closer and my eyes widened. He looked exactly the same as he did twenty-five years ago. Siren's father, Leo, was staring at me through the mirror.

"I-I... um, yea that's just a little game we play," I started, but Siren dropped her head and her mother burst into laughter.

This was awkward as shit. I scratched my head. "Uh, Leo, how you been, man?" I asked, trying to be casual.

He smirked. "Better now that I've seen my wife and kids. I can rest a little easier now. Thank you for protecting them, especially Siren. She's hot headed like her mother."

Both Siren and mother rolled their eyes." I hear you're making a good mate," he finally smiled.

I breathed a little easier, glad that he was okay with everything. "I would lay down my life for her," I told him honestly.

He nodded his head, thanked the Gods, and focused his attention on Willow. Mike walked out of the bathroom, smirking at me. I assumed he heard everything. He paid respects to Leo, gave me dap, and headed downstairs. Siren then excused herself to give her mom and dad some privacy. She grabbed my hand and led me to the balcony. She loved sitting out here because of the view of the garden, pool, and woods. Sometimes, she would come out here late at night when she thought everyone was asleep and I'd watch her, watching the stars. She looked at me and giggled.

"Hey, daddy," she whispered.

I laughed, "You know who daddy is, right?" I quizzed.

"Uhmm hmmm," she moaned and dropped to her knees.

I let her unzip me and take me into her mouth. Her oral skills still amazed me. I was in heaven when I was in her mouth. Before she could pull the nut up from my toes, I quickly snatched her up. Lifting her, I prepared to rip the crotch of her jeans, but she stopped me.

"I want to show you something," she said in a seductive voice. She snapped her fingers and our clothes disappeared.

"Perfect," I growled, reaching for her again.

"Wait! That's not all," she said, giggling and batting my hands away. I was becoming impatient and I slowly started walking toward her. Before I could reach her, she started to shimmer and become transparent.

She flickered in and out while I looked at her, confused. Suddenly in a cloud of white light, she split into two. I was looking at two naked Sirens. My jaw hit the floor. She spun around, and so did the other

Siren. She played with her titties and slid her hand down to her pussy, and so did the other Siren. I didn't think it was possible for my dick to be as hard as it was. She whispered something in her ear, and one Siren went down to finish sucking my dick while the other ran her nails over my chest and tongue-kissed me deeply. At this point, I didn't know who was who. I ended up pounding both of them in every position imaginable, until we were all exhausted. I laid on the bed with a Siren on each arm, until she snapped her fingers and one disappeared.

"Damn," I said out of breath. "Are these the perks of mating with a witch?" She grinned and nodded her head.

Before long, she dozed off and I got up to take a shower. Our master bathroom mimicked outside. All the walls were made of exotic plants, and the shower head was made like a waterfall. We even had a built in Jacuzzi, surrounded by shrubs that looked like a babbling brook. Siren decorated everything. She was in the process of starting her own interior decorating business. She insisted she needed something of her own, despite the fact that I had long money from years of investments. I was proud of her and knew she would be wonderful at it. Stepping under the waterfall, I enjoyed the hot water running over my muscles. The buzzing from my phone pulled me out of my thoughts. It was an urgent text from my contact in Boston. I'd have to go there in a few days to make sure everything was straight. I wrapped a giant hunter green towel around my waist and headed to the kitchen.

"Alright nigga, do I gotta start putting my name on my food?" I asked July, who was digging into the deer I killed earlier. He looked up with blood smeared all over his face.

"My bad, Mega. I checked the fridge first, but it was nothing but steak. We been having steak since we been here. Besides, I didn't want this going to waste seeing as though you were... occupied," he finished with a smirk.

Shaking my head, I chuckled and broke off one of the back legs, then stood over the sink munching. "I gotta go to Boston in a few days," I told July.

"What they fuckin' up now?" he asked.

"Nothing. Just a transfer of alpha." I shrugged. Sensing something was wrong, he raised his brow, "Want me to go with you?"

I shook my head. "Nah, I need you here. To keep an eye on Siren. Something still ain't sitting right with me with this Dame nigga. I don't trust him," I said.

He nodded his head, "Say no more," he assured me and dug back into the deer.

I cleaned the bone, washed my hands, and headed back upstairs. I laid next to Siren, and she immediately cuddled into me and threw her heavy ass leg over mine. I drifted off to sleep, content.

20

SIREN

*I*t had been two days since Mega left for Boston. I was missing him like crazy, and I still had a week to go. Shit, I should've just went with him. I could've visited Salem. I'd always wanted to do a little conjure work there, but I just started my business, *Wild Homes Interior Decorating*. You can't see me, but I'm bowing right now because I assume you're clapping for me. My goal with the business is to bring touches of nature inside your home and blend it with chic decor. I just had my first client, Mrs. Allen, who was actually the wife of the real estate agent who first showed us this house. They came to check how we were doing after we'd been here a few days. She was amazed over my bathroom and insisted I do hers. You know what my first check looked like after a few sketches, a little work, and a few magic fingers? Twenty percent went to Gee since she sketched out my ideas to show the client before I started. That chick quit her part time job ASAP and declared herself my official sketch artist. Of course, Mrs. Allen told all her wealthy friends, and I was now booked solid for the next two months.

It felt good to have something I liked to keep me busy and my mind occupied. Sometimes, I felt myself become sad as the empty feeling of the pup I lost would consume me. I tried my hardest not to think about it, especially since I wasn't even sure if I was ready to be somebody's mother in the first place. Whenever I would conjure my dad, he always assured me that the pup was safe with him and he would send him back when the time was right. I took solace in that. I noticed my mom's powers were coming back a little stronger as well. She didn't think I knew, but she was calling my dad up almost every day because he told me. Sometimes, he would cut our time short because she called him. I didn't mind. Their time was cut short on this realm, so shit, they might as well enjoy themselves now. If my mother wanted to carry on an affair with a ghost, more power to her. Mike had really surprised me. He moved in and cut off all his hoes for my girl. I'm sure he was going to do that even before I threatened to cut his dick off, put a bow on it, and give it to Gee as a gift if he fucked her over.

They had even been talking about turning her into a shifter so they could officially mate. That shit would be dope, for real, to have another female shifter here. They made each other happy, and that made me happy. Don't get it twisted though, Gee was still the hood anchorwoman. We got up every morning and sat on our combined deck, and she always poured me that piping hot tea. July decided to stay with us, and I had grown to like him a lot. We all did. He was like an honorary member of the family. If anybody was having a bad day and happened to bump into him around the house, he would have your ass cracking up at whatever he decided to point out that day.

Like the day Gee got her bundles caught in the door and this nigga told her it was the spirits of all the horses who ever got locked in a barn. Even after she explained to him that it wasn't horse hair, he stuck to his theory of horse spirits. I said it before, that nigga is a fool. I secretly made it my mission to find him a girl because although he joked a lot, everyone had those lonely times. So here we were, the four of us, all dressed up to go celebrate the first gig for my business, and the guys were pissed at us because Gee and I wanted to go to our favorite spot... Ruby Tuesday's.

"Y'all ain't got no class. You broads mean to tell me, you started a business where all yo' checks is five figures or more and y'all wanna go to... Ruby Tuesdays?" July said, frowning his face up.

"No class? Coming from the nigga that bite his toenails in the kitchen," Gee said, pointing at his feet.

"Ewwwww, July! In the kitchen! Where we eat?" I screeched.

Gee shot me side eye 'cause she knew what me and Mega did in the kitchen on a daily basis, so I quickly shut my mouth before she told my business.

"Come on, sis! My treat! Pick one of the best steak houses you can think of," Mike said, trying to change my mind.

"No steak!" July yelled.

I chuckled and shrugged my shoulders, "Welp, looks like Ruby Tuesday's it is!" I said, linking arms with Gee as we skipped out the door while the guys grumbled behind us.

Mega took me to fancy spots all the time, but it was so rare that I got to just hang out and do hood rat shit with my hood rat friend. I climbed in the back of my brother's BMW, trying not to show my pussy in the little black body-con dress I wore. I was feeling like a ghetto superstar as we bumped Future and put some weed in the air on the way to the restaurant.

ONCE WE WERE SEATED and ordered almost every appetizer on the menu, our main courses and a host of different drinks, we chatted amongst ourselves. Guess who decided to walk their ass on over to the table... Jerry, the virgin! This must be his hangout too.

"Hey! I remember you! You never called! Us virgins have to stick together!" he said, loud as ever.

"I'm sorry, Jerry. I'm no longer a part of that club. My pussy been beat on more than an African drum," I said, taking a sip of my fruity drink and causing his light face to turn about nine different shades of red.

"What the fuck, Si?" my brother shouted angrily, choking on his drink while Gee screamed in laughter. "I'm going to the bathroom to throw up," Mike said, making us laugh harder.

"Wait for me, bro," July said, getting up, "Your sister nasty as fuck," he said, catching up with Mike. Jerry had scurried away, leaving me and Gee to continue cackling.

"Good one, bitch!" she said, high-fiving me.

"I know, right! And I just thought it up on the spot!" I bragged on my wittiness.

We quickly tossed back some shots and as I slammed my glass to the table, I almost choked from who I saw in my peripheral vision.

"Hey-hey, Dame," I stuttered. It was like he'd magically appeared at our table.

I quickly looked him over. Although I wasn't comfortable with him taking over Green River because of the vision I had at that last meeting, I made sure that he and his brothers were constantly under my protection by sending one of my heavy hitter ancestors to guide him daily, and I had to admit, shifting fit him well. His light brown skin was flawless and possessed a slight glow. His eyes which were normally honey colored now looked like honey in the sunshine with spots of gold and amber flecked through them. His waves were deep, and his beard was shiny. He was a little bigger, slightly more muscular than he already was, but he still had his baby face. I sniffed very lightly, not wanting him to know what I was doing, and his scent was crazy. It was the scent he already had, but it was magnified and of course, I could smell his Armani code and it was electrifying my body.

He smiled, showing his dimple as he twirled a toothpick around his mouth. He leaned on the table, close to me and took a big whiff, making it obvious that he was sniffing me, which would be considered disrespectful since I was already mated.

"Sexy Siren, I missed you," he said, running a finger along my jaw. "What's up Gee?" he said, glancing at her.

I stole that moment to force myself to breathe since apparently, I'd forgotten I was supposed to be doing that. Gee kicked me under the table, and I'm sure her hard ass pumps were going to leave an indentation in my leg as she nervously looked toward the restrooms before speaking to him.

He chuckled. "Don't worry, I saw when them niggas dipped off. I just wanted to come see my future wifey," he said, looking at me again. "Congrats on the business, I saw it on Instagram. I just got a new crib and it needs a woman's touch, so Imma need your services," he said, removing the toothpick from his mouth. "I'll be in touch," he whispered in my ear before sniffing me again, adjusting his pants on his waist and walking off. He was looking like a trap god. He left just seconds before the guys returned to the table. Gee was watching me with wide eyes while I bit my lip and nervously pulled apart a mozzarella stick as the guys sat down. I kept my thighs clenched tightly together, praying that no one could smell my arousal.

"I hope you're done talking about your pussy because—" Mike started. but stopped in the middle of his sentence as he sniffed the air.

July cut into his chicken and said, "So, that nigga waited until we dipped off before he crept over here," he said, unbothered, never looking up from his plate.

I released a breath, glad that it was Dame's scent in the air that they were smelling and not me. Mike looked around, and July motioned his head to the back. We all turned and Dame, Marsean and Amauri sat at a booth in the back with all types of paperwork over the table. Looked like a business meeting. Mike eyed me and then looked to Gee, who was now fiddling with her phone.

"So, nobody gonna say shit!" he finally yelled, causing Gee to jump a little.

I sighed, "He saw the business on the 'gram, so he came over to say congratulations," I said, shrugging my shoulders, telling a half truth and knowing Gee wouldn't say anything.

For the next few minutes, all I could hear were forks and knives clinking against our plates because it was so quiet, until finally Gee said.

"I wanna go somewhere and dance. Come on, y'all," she tugged

Mike's arm and covertly shot me a look. He reached into his pocket and produced enough cash to cover the bill and enough for a nice tip.

Gee and Mike stood from the table and I started to follow, but July grabbed my wrist.

"Whatever you thinking, don't do it," he said seriously.

"I'm not thinking anything! He's an ex, that's all," I said.

"Keep it that way. Mega has been real calm lately, trust me, you want to keep him that way," he said.

I nodded and stood to adjust my little black dress. I don't know why, but I glanced in Dame's direction. He was staring right at me. He discreetly puckered his full moist lips and blew me a kiss before I turned. I put my head down and smiled to myself before hurrying to catch up with Mike and Gee. Fuck my life.

21

JADE THE SUCCUBUS

*H*ey, guys. I wanted to tell you a little bit about myself, other than I'm a cock sucker from hell. I'm really so much more. I want to be an actress. I've had dreams of my face gracing the big screen ever since movies were only black and white. Not porn, but like an actual Halle Berry cry face, accepting my award actress. And, I think this is the perfect millennia to do it. I'd be perfect on a show like *Empire* or *Power*— hell, even *Insecure!* If the most well-known family of succubi, the Kardashian, could acquire fame, so could I. As far as my personal life goes, I'm in love with Malachi Black, the boss of the black cartel. He's the only man that I've ever loved, but trust, I'm not like Siren. I have sex with my man all the time. I just make sure I'm already full on souls before I make love to him, so I won't drive him crazy. When he called me and told me his little brothers were on a dummy mission against some shifter and he needed my help, I didn't hesitate to lure Bear over to the bar. I would've killed his ass if he wasn't so strong. Mere mortals never stand a chance, but the others could be a little tougher. You win some and you lose some, but at least I drained him enough to put him on his ass. A discombobulated beast is easier to kill when he is at his strongest capacity. Any who, I'll make sure Siren's ass doesn't hog all the chapters and I'll be sure to have a larger part next time, and I can take you in depth a little more. Don't be a stranger. Catch you in Bellmont in book two. Smooches.

To Be Continued.

Coming 05/14!

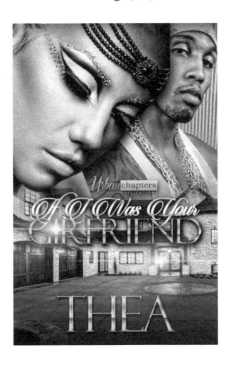

CPSIA information can be obtained
at www.ICGtesting.com
Printed in the USA
LVHW05s1944200618
581394LV00021B/415/P